Rearmed and Dangerous

Longarm threw himself out of his saddle, hitting the ground on both feet and facing the horse. He fell back from the pitching, rearing buckskin and, glancing left, saw the butt of his own rifle protruding from Dixon's jouncing saddle boot.

As the roar of a shotgun rose from the other side of the grave and a revolver popped, men yelling and horses screaming, hooves thudding and tack squawking, Longarm wrapped his left hand around the rifle's butt, gave it a jerk, then threw himself right to avoid the claybank's kicking rear hooves.

He hit the ground on a shoulder and, jacking a round into the Winchester's breech, angled the barrel upward . . .

TABOR EVANS

LONGARM

AND THE DIAMOND SISTERS

J

JOVE BOOKS, NEW YORK

THE BERKLEY PUBLISHING GROUP
Published by the Penguin Group
Penguin Group (USA) Inc.
375 Hudson Street, New York, New York 10014, USA
Penguin Group (Canada), 90 Eglinton Avenue East, Suite 700, Toronto, Ontario M4P 2Y3, Canada
(a division of Pearson Penguin Canada Inc.)
Penguin Books Ltd., 80 Strand, London WC2R 0RL, England
Penguin Group Ireland, 25 St. Stephen's Green, Dublin 2, Ireland (a division of Penguin Books Ltd.)
Penguin Group (Australia), 250 Camberwell Road, Camberwell, Victoria 3124, Australia
(a division of Pearson Australia Group Pty. Ltd.)
Penguin Books India Pvt. Ltd., 11 Community Centre, Panchsheel Park, New Delhi—110 017, India
Penguin Group (NZ), 67 Apollo Drive, Rosedale, North Shore 0632, New Zealand
(a division of Pearson New Zealand Ltd.)
Penguin Books (South Africa) (Pty.) Ltd., 24 Sturdee Avenue, Rosebank, Johannesburg 2196,
South Africa

Penguin Books Ltd., Registered Offices: 80 Strand, London WC2R 0RL, England

This is a work of fiction. Names, characters, places, and incidents either are the product of the author's imagination or are used fictitiously, and any resemblance to actual persons, living or dead, business establishments, events, or locales is entirely coincidental.

LONGARM AND THE DIAMOND SISTERS

A Jove Book / published by arrangement with the author

PRINTING HISTORY
Jove edition / July 2008

Copyright © 2008 by The Berkley Publishing Group.
Cover illustration by Miro Sinovcic.

ISBN: 978-0-515-14482-6

JOVE®
Jove Books are published by The Berkley Publishing Group,
a division of Penguin Group (USA) Inc.,
375 Hudson Street, New York, New York 10014.
JOVE is a registered trademark of Penguin Group (USA) Inc.
The "J" design is a trademark belonging to Penguin Group (USA) Inc.

PRINTED IN THE UNITED STATES OF AMERICA

10 9 8 7 6 5 4 3 2 1

Chapter 1

Deputy Sheriff Sylvus Judd's voice trembled as he squinted down into the valley before him. "That 'Loony Larry' Dixon—he'll send you to the Great Hereafter in little bitty pieces on a hot shovel." He shook his bearded head. "My bowels all been tied in a knot ever since he rode into the country, and I keep streakin' my drawers!"

Heck Longtree, Sheriff of Snakehead Gap, Colorado Territory, chuckled as he squatted beside Judd, who was staring into the same hollow and holding his Spencer repeater butt down against the ground. He ran a finger across his long, salt-and-pepper mustache and spat into the grama grass waving in the breeze before him. "Shit, Sylvus. Loony Larry bleeds same as us. If Loony Larry is who you seen, and not a ghost."

"Oh, it's him, all right, Sheriff. That's the man we seen on the fresh batch of Wanted dodgers. I'd bet my right oyster on it." Sylvus Judd sniffed. "Maybe he does bleed same as us. But there's been damn little proof. I heard tell he was a hardened outlaw and cold-steel artist for about twelve years before he went to prison up in Montana Territory, and was never shot once!"

"Luck of the pure evil—that's all it is," Longtree said, gritting his teeth as he cocked the Spencer. He was a big, pot-bellied, hollow-cheeked man clad in a moth-eaten yellow duster over a brown wool vest and duck trousers, the cuffs of which were stuffed into the tops of his stovepipe boots. "If that really is his coyote dun down there—and if that *really is* Loony Larry ridin' it—I'll soon be provin' my point, Sylvus. Less'n he gives himself up, that is. And, from what you've told me about that kill-crazy son of a bitch, he don't *do* that."

"That's his horse, all right," Judd said, squeezing the old Spencer repeater in his age-gnarled hands. "I trailed him out from town one night. I'd recognize that big dun anywhere. Just like I recognized its tracks."

Judd was pushing sixty and, since the crime rate was generally low not only in Snakehead Gap but in all of Hatchet Woman County, he was Longtree's sole deputy and spent most of his time running a little chicken and pig farm on the outskirts of town.

He and Sheriff Longtree had ridden out toward the Diamond Bar B ranch to investigate several killings that had occurred around Snakehead Gap since the hombre who looked like Loony Larry had appeared in the country. They'd cut the tracks of the big dun, with one cracked shoe, just north of Hatchet Woman Creek and followed them here.

The long-legged, broad-chested dun stood beside a saddled paint at the hitch rack fronting a crude plank, brush-roofed cabin flanked by a roofless privy. The cabin sat at the edge of a thin copse of burr oaks and piñon pines rising over low hills, with a dry, rocky lake bed stretching out before it. A muddy stream, chuckling and glittering in the mid-afternoon sunshine, split the lake bed down the middle, about fifty yards beyond the cabin's dilapidated front stoop.

"Damn good work, Sylvus. Damn good work," said Sheriff Longtree as he studied the cabin. "I'd much rather shake down old Loony Larry with as few others around as possible. If Howard Diamond has one gunslick workin' for him, he probably has more."

"Who do you think belongs to that other horse?" the deputy asked, canting his head at the paint drawing water from the stock trough beneath the hitch rack.

"You pay better attention to the ridin' stock around here than I do," Longtree said, grunting as he pushed up off his knees. "You don't recognize it?"

"No, sir. Probably another of the Diamond Bar B boys. I just hope it ain't another gunslick. Just thinkin' about dealin' with ole Loony Larry's got me ready to squirt green shit down the inside of my pants leg."

"Don't worry, Sylvus," the sheriff chuckled. "It's always been my policy, when dealin' with men faster and meaner'n me—which includes practically all the men I've ever arrested—to sneak up on 'em and gain the element of surprise. And, if necessary, just to go ahead and back-shoot the sons of bitches. Fuck pride. There's plenty of proud men taking harp lessons in heaven."

Staring into the hollow, Longtree snatched a tobacco braid from inside his corduroy jacket, bit off a sizable plug, then replaced the braid. Chewing with his mouth open, he tapped his deputy's shoulder. "Let's go down and take the bull by the horns."

Sylvus Judd cursed under his breath as he followed about ten feet behind Longtree, hoofing it north along the ridge crest, both men careful that the sky didn't outline them, then dropped down the ridge into a copse of widely spaced bullberry shrubs and spindly cottonwoods. The trees would shield the lawmen from anyone looking out the cabin's windows, and from the horses who might whinny a warning.

Finding a game path littered with deer pellets and a pan-sized plop of two-day-old bear shit, Longtree zigzagged down the slope. At the bottom, he paused to scan the cabin once more.

Spying no movement in the windows, he tapped the edgy Judd's shoulder, grinned cunningly, then ran, crouching and holding his rifle low in his right hand, through the buffeting bluestem and wild timothy to the cabin's back wall.

Judd followed, running as fast as his old legs would carry him in his stovepipe boots, from which he'd removed his spurs back where he and the sheriff had left their horses. He pulled up behind the crude shack, beside Longtree, and raking air in and out of his aching lungs, dropped to one knee and pulled at the grass.

"Gonna make it, Sylvus?" said the sheriff, squinting one eye at him wryly, though he, too, was sucking air down his lungs.

"I'll make—" The old deputy stopped and, frowning, turned his head slightly to one side. He'd heard a sound from within the cabin's thin walls, and it came again now—a man's deep-throated groan followed by a girl's laugh.

Judd looked at Longtree. The sheriff was frowning up at the window over Judd's head. He canted his head toward the other window on the near end of the shack, and Judd, crouching, scampered over and hunkered down beneath it. When Longtree was snugged up against the first window, the men exchanged conspiratorial glances.

The sheriff doffed his hat, and nodded.

Judd removed his own hat, then rose slowly, edging a look up over the window's sun-blistered sash and through one warped, dusty pane.

Staring hard through the glass, his own shadow blocking the sun's reflection, he cast his gaze around the inside of the cabin. It was furnished with a few sticks of rough-hewn furniture, saddle blankets and tack hanging from joists and beams, and a black sheet-iron stove against the left wall, flanked by a wood box. Against the right wall was a cot, and on the cot sat a naked man, leaning back against the wall. A naked girl knelt between the man's spread knees, moving her head slowly up and down, her mouth draped over the man's jutting cock.

The man was lean and hard-bodied, with tattoos up and down his arms and across his chest. The top of his head was bald, but long, white hair hung down from the sides, and a slender braid fell across a shoulder from the back. He slowly rolled his head from side to side, lower jaw hanging, groaning.

To his right, a sawed-off double-barreled shotgun lay across the cot.

Judd couldn't see much of the girl from this angle, but he could tell it was Aubrey Diamond, with her gold blond hair piled like spun honey atop her beautiful head. Her clothes and Loony Larry Dixon's were spread across the cabin's earthen floor.

The girl suddenly lifted her head, making wet sucking sounds Sylvus could hear through the window. She looked up at the man. "Do you like that, Larry?"

"Goddamnit," Loony Larry said, gritting his teeth,

placing his big, pale hands on both sides of the girl's head, and pulling it back down to his cock. "Keep goin'! I'll tell you when to stop!"

The girl gave a startled grunt, then choked and gagged as the man's cock was rammed back into her mouth.

Heart thudding and loins aching, Sylvus Judd pulled his head back from the window. He glanced over at Sheriff Longtree. The sheriff beckoned to him, a strained look on the lawman's face. Sylvus grabbed his rifle and, keeping his head low, crabbed over to Longtree.

"We got the bastard right where we want him!" Longtree rasped, shoulders jerking as he restrained a chuckle. "Let's go!"

Longtree stole around the corner and along the cabin's east side, holding his Winchester up high across his chest. Judd moved along behind him, heart thudding, still hearing Loony Larry's moans and groans behind the thin wall to his left.

Longtree turned the cabin's front corner and tiptoed along the dilapidated porch to the front door, cooing softly to the horses tied to the hitch rack. They were eyeing Longtree and Judd warily, twitching their ears.

Inside, Loony Larry was moaning even louder than before. "Yeah, that's it," he exclaimed. "That's it . . . that's the way . . . oh, sweet *mercy*!"

As Judd crept along the porch, aiming his Spencer repeater straight out from his right hip, Sheriff Longtree smoothed down his sweat-soaked mustache with one hand and turned to the door.

"Yeah, baby," Loony Larry intoned on the other side of the front wall. "Oh, Jesus, yeah . . . there you go. You got the rhythm now, girl!"

Longtree glanced at Judd, who froze about ten feet

east of the door. The sheriff grinned devilishly, then squared his shoulders and, holding his rifle straight up and down in both hands, raised his right foot waist-high, heel out. He'd just started thrusting his boot toward the door when a thunderlike blast sounded and a pumpkin-sized hole appeared in the door planks, wood slivers flying in every direction.

KA-BOOOM!

Sheriff Ned Longtree screamed as he bounded two feet up in the air and, as though caught in a whistling prairie cyclone, flew straight back between the two horses to hit the ground in a fog of billowing dust and careening wood slivers.

The horses nickered and whinnied and skitter-stepped away from the sheriff, who, Judd saw as he gaped through the sifting dust, lay on his back, showing a hole the same size as the one in the door gaping and gushing blood in the dead center of his chest.

Longtree groaned and moved his hands and arms as though doing a backstroke in some quiet prairie stock pond, but the movement soon turned to spasms. The sheriff lifted his dusty, hatless head, stretched his lips back from his teeth, then grunted, threw his head back in the dust between the two nervous horses, and lay still.

Blood welled up from his chest like water from a spring and turned the ground beneath him black as tar.

Something moved in the left periphery of Judd's swimming vision. He turned abruptly toward the cabin door.

A man stood in the open doorway—a pale, naked man with long, white hair curling onto his broad, pale shoulders. The top of the man's head was bald as a baby's ass, his eyes were the gray blue of a lake on a cloudy day, and in his arms he held a sawed-off, double-barreled barn blaster.

Both maws yawned at Judd's belly. Gray smoke curled from the right barrel. The left was black as a moonless night.

"Ah, shit," the deputy moaned.

He had his rifle turned toward the dead sheriff. Even if he hadn't turned to stone the moment he'd seen the sheriff fly out from the cabin in a swarm of steel pellets, smoke, and wood splinters, he couldn't have brought the rifle around in time to beat the finger of Loony Larry Dixon, which was curled over the trigger of the gut shredder's left trigger.

"Ah, shit," Judd moaned again.

Soft footsteps rose in the cabin's shadows, and a naked girl swam up out of the darkness to stand in the doorway beside Dixon.

She was a tall, big-boned girl, with broad hips and large upturned breasts the color of fresh whipped cream. Honey blond hair swam about her shoulders. She had a mole on her chin, another above her left eyebrow.

As her violet eyes swept across the sheriff lying dead in the dust before the porch, she smiled to Deputy Sheriff Judd standing frozen and dribbling water down the inside of his left pants leg. She snaked an arm around Loony Larry's waist and rested her chin on his shoulder.

She reached out and, keeping her eyes on Judd, ran her free hand down the shotgun's broad barrels—from the end to the rabbit-eared hammers and halfway back again. She shuddered. Gooseflesh rose on her breasts and shoulders. Her pink nipples pebbled.

"Do it, Larry," she said huskily, staring at Judd. "I wanna watch you do it."

Loony Larry Dixon spread a grim smile inside the thick, white mustache drooping down both corners of his wide, pink mouth.

"Okay," he said.

The shotgun roared.

Chapter 2

"Nuthin' like a Fourth of July celebration, eh, Custis?" said Chief Marshal Billy Vail as he watched the parade passing along cobbled, sun-splashed Colfax Avenue before him. "Parades, pretty gals in new frocks, barking dogs, fireworks, ice cream, and brass horns. Why, I feel so dang patriotic, I'm getting gooseflesh all up and down my spine!"

"Me, too, Chief," said Deputy U.S. Marshal Custis Long, known far and wide to friend and foe as Longarm. Sucking one of his three-for-a-nickel cheroots and rising up on the toes of his stovepipe cavalry boots, he peered out across the parade of fat, gaudily clad Lutheran Church League women raising wood-handled signs that touted the merits of a chaste, liquor-free Denver. The deputy's steel gray eyes gleamed lustily out from beneath the flat brim of the snuff brown hat tipped at a rakish angle over his right brow.

"Oh, yeah," Longarm said, when he found what he was looking for on the other side of the street. "Me—I got that gooseflesh all over me, Chief. Got it so bad it hurts."

Chief Vail glanced up at the long, rangy drink of water who was not only the best lawman in his stable but the best lawman he'd ever known—though he wouldn't have admitted that to Longarm if Apaches were slow roasting him on a wagon wheel spit and basting him every five minutes with tizwin spiced with fire ants.

The chief marshal followed the deputy's gaze across the street, spying a girl with blond sausage curls—seventeen or eighteen years old and decked out in a low-cut, form-fitting, red, white, and blue cotton dress with matching parasol. A comely lass, her proud, creamy breasts threatened to spill out of their tight, spare, lace-edged harness. Facing Longarm and twirling the parasol while grinning like the cat that ate the canary, she seemed bound and determined to make them do just that.

Unfortunately for Longarm, the girl's arm was hooked through the arm of a dapper young gent in a crisp beaver hat with a mustache waxed to a saberlike edge.

"Yeah, that's just about as patriotic a getup as one might don on one's bosomy frame," allowed Billy Vail, lifting his brown bowler to scratch his bald, pink pate. "But before you get any ideas about hoofin' it over there to throw your own calling card in the girl's basket, I must inform you she's the daughter of the governor's top aide—a very wealthy aide with digs up on Sherman Street not far from General Larimer himself—and the gentleman leading her around on a short rope is the son of a wealthy haberdasher from Piney Dale, Ohio."

"Damn," Longarm said, hands on his hips as he chewed his half-smoked cheroot. The dandy was pulling the girl off through the crowd, but having noticed Longarm ogling her shamelessly—as he was wont to do when he spied an object of his profound desire—she turned her head to hold his gaze, offering a toothy, dimpled smile, blue eyes flashing like sequins in the sunlight. "That just burns me right to the core, Chief. It purely does. A face like that, tits like that, wasted on a storekeeper's tinhorn son."

Billy scowled up at the big lawman. "She's too young for you, anyway."

"You know what they say, Chief . . ."

"Don't say it. We're in public. You're a lawman of distinction, however dubious, having been written up in both the *Rocky Mountain News* and the *Illustrated Police Gazette*, and you need to start acting pure and proper as the church choir unless you want my eight-and-a-half brogan shoved so far up your ass it'll take a dentist and two hod carriers to extract it."

"Well, excuse me all to hell while I go home and shine my badge."

"Ah, shit."

Longarm glanced down at the short, plump lawman in his rumpled suit and dusty bowler. Billy Vail was scowling down the street past Longarm's right shoulder, through the milling crowd of families, tail-wagging dogs, and crippled Civil War veterans. Occasionally, a firecracker popped amidst the off-key strains of the brass band playing under a roofed gazebo not fifty yards away on the lawn of the Federal Mint.

"What is it, Chief? The wife and kids?"

"Nah. I left them and my mother-in-law in the park yonder with a kite and a basket of fried chicken. The wife's ridin' the old broomstick again—breaks out in thimble-sized hives at the sight of me." Still looking off through the crowd, Billy shaped a wooden smile on his round, pudgy face and raised his arm to wave. "It's the good general and that niece of his you've been using for a human pincushion."

Longarm wheeled, grinning. Maybe the day could be saved, after all. Sure enough, heading right toward them strode the regal, leonine-headed, old General Larimer himself, founding father of Denver, and the niece he prized more than all his Thoroughbreds and Tennessee walkers combined. Longarm prized Miss Cynthia Larimer, because—in spite of her ceaselessly imploring him to escort her to such torturous cultural shindigs as Shakespearian plays, operas, masquerade balls, and even a couple of Russian ballets—she was the most masterful, creative, and athletic lover he'd ever known.

In fact, after a night in the girl's boudoir—or atop the general's desk or in the Larimers' marble-floored foyer or stables or rose garden or astride one of the general's beloved stallions—Longarm felt as though he could die right then and there and not feel as though he'd missed a damn thing . . . that he had, in fact, squeezed out every drop life had to offer.

"Well, if it isn't Marshals Vail and Long!" the general roared like an old grizzly fresh out of its hibernation cave. "Look, Cynthia, I told you it was them!"

Guffawing, the general released the girl's slim-fingered hand, shuffled his horse-head, silver-plated walking stick to his left palm, and extended his right hand, on the middle finger of which a Corinthian scrolls onyx and diamond ring flashed and winked in the sunlight.

"Good to see you, Marshal Vail. Deputy Long, always nice to see my dear Cynthia's protector. Billy, this is my

14

niece Cynthia from Cambridge and various other points of the worldly compass. A real world traveler, she, but a couple times every year she suffers a visit to her old uncle, and I couldn't be more pleased when she does!"

Billy bowed slightly at his broad waist and squeezed the girl's hand in his own. "How could I ever forget such a pretty face? Miss Larimer, welcome back to Denver."

"And I know you remember Cynthia, Deputy Long," said the general, laughing heartily.

Billy cast Longarm a surreptitious, vaguely castigating glance as the general continued, "How could you forget the young lady who, every time she's in town, coerces you into leading her around to all those tawdry, stuffy social and *artistic* affairs of hers?"

The girl was tall, regal, even stately, while teeming with a ball-burning sensuality. Flowing down from beneath a small straw hat trimmed with ostrich feathers and fake chokecherry blossoms, her hair was long, shiny, and black as a Sioux princess's. Long full lips shaped a sexy mouth. Her cheeks were like Longtree-sculpted marble, and the eyes, set wide above a straight, long nose, were the color of melted chocolate.

Those eyes held Longarm's gaze. The cool, dusty look under thin, dark brows, coupled with the pale breasts pushing up from her low-cut, lace-edged, pink frock, gave Longarm an instant hard-on.

Allowing his eyes only a momentary gander at the bewitching orbs he'd kneaded and licked until the girl had howled like a horny she-wolf, Longarm gave a friendly bow and resisted the urge to pant. The girl had been groomed from birth to be wed to a male of her social station, and if the general ever got wind she'd been coupling

15

with a mongrel like Longarm, he'd no doubt suffer a stroke—and probably have Longarm drawn, quartered, and horsewhipped before sending the girl to a convent in South America.

"Nice to see you again, Miss Larimer," Longarm said, carefully pitching his voice with appropriate warmth and friendliness rather than lust. "I didn't know you were back in Colorado."

"Just picked her up at the train station an hour ago," the general said, beaming.

"Unfortunately, I'm only here for a couple of days, Custis," Cynthia said with the practiced reserve she used only in the presence of the general and the general's cheery, full-hipped wife, Fannie. "I was going to call on you, but since you didn't answer any of the notes I sent, I was afraid you considered me a bother."

Longarm frowned. "Notes? What notes?"

"Oh, I sent several to your office," the girl said. "One from Philadelphia, one from Detroit . . . you mean, you didn't *receive* them?" The girl turned her cool, suspicious gaze to Billy Vail, as did Longarm. The chief marshal dropped his own eyes to the sidewalk, stuffed his hands in his pockets, and cleared his throat nervously.

"Uh . . . well, if you sent them to the Federal Building, Miss Larimer, no tellin' what happened to them. While I run my own office tight as a Norwegian clipper ship, who knows what goes on in the mail room?" Billy chuckled like the boy who left the snake in the girls' privy. "Anyway, you say you're in town for only a few days? Ah, that's a shame!"

"A day or two," Longarm said, casting his boss another castigating glance. "You know me, Miss Cynthia—anything I can do to be of service to the general's niece . . ."

16

Cynthia sucked her fingertip with practiced coyness and slit her beguiling eyes. "Hmm. I was planning on attending a piano recital tomorrow. Since you didn't get my letters"—her cool, subtly castigating eyes darted to Billy once more—"I wasn't sure whom I was going to get to take me . . ."

"Piano recital, eh?" Longarm said.

Cynthia had a habbit of dragging him to events he wouldn't have dreamed of attending with anyone less adept at rewarding him for his efforts, but something told him that, since her time was limited, she had no intention of hauling him out to a piano recital. They'd no doubt meet secretly somewhere—at the Silver Lady Hotel, for instance—and fuck like dogs in a canopied, four-poster between courses of roasted duck or grilled chicken and bottles of French wine.

"Well," Longarm said, feigning reticence, "those Chopin tunes do tend to grow on a feller . . ."

"You'll take me, then?" Cynthia said, casting a furtive glance at her uncle, who stood with a slightly amused smile on his broad, bearded face, his blue eyes a tad watery, no doubt from furtive sips from a brandy flask. "I've heard the city has, in spite of the best efforts of the local police force, grown rather wooly around the edges," Cynthia said. "I wouldn't dare venture out unattended!"

Billy Vail cleared his throat. "Afraid I'm gonna have to step in here, Miss Larimer. I hate to rain on your parade, but unfortunately, I'll be sending Longar—I mean, Deputy Long—out to the northwest corner of the state first thing tomorrow morning. Hairy job up thataway. Rustlers and such. No tellin' how long he'll be gone."

Longarm and Cynthia scowled at Billy. "Chief, you didn't say anything about—"

"I'm sorry, Custis," Billy said, rising up on the balls of his feet, flipping his hat in his hands, giving a terrible portrayal of a deeply regretful boss. "Totally slipped my overworked mind, I reckon. Sure enough, bad business up north. Only my best man will do for an assignment of such gravity. My apologies, Miss Larimer. General, perhaps you could find *another* escort for your niece, since it's just so dang unfortunate that Deputy Long here will be out of town on assignment for at least two weeks."

"Well, there you have it, my dear," the general said, patting the girl's hand. "We'll simply have to find someone else, that's all. Let me consult my associates."

Cynthia's voice was cool as she addressed Billy. "You're sure there's no one else you could send, Marshal? I do feel *so* safe in Deputy Long's company."

"I'm afraid there's just no chance, Miss Larimer," Billy said, rising again on the balls of his feet and looking off sheepishly. "Terribly sorry, terribly sorry."

"Well, in that case," the girl said, putting on a brave face but giving Billy Vail a vaguely peevish look, "I guess I'll just have to find someone else. I certainly wouldn't want to stand in the way of law and order up north."

"There, there, my dear," the general said. "I'm sure we'll find someone else to fill Longarm's shoes. In fact, I know a retired policeman—I believe his name's O'Toole. Nearly my own age, I'm afraid, but a right capable sort."

Cynthia cast Longarm an ironic glance. "O'Toole. Yes, I'm sure he'll fill Longarm's shoes in every way."

Longarm's face heated up. "Sorry, Miss Larimer," he said quickly, to cover a stillborn chuckle. "It does appear I'm a little tied up. Next time, you'd best send your letters to my home address, bypass the office altogether, so I can clear my schedule for you."

"I'll do that, Deputy." Cynthia cordially extended her hand. "It was nice seeing you again. Until next time I'm in Denver . . ."

"I'll be ready and rarin' to join you for any *piano recital* you name," Longarm said, shaking the girl's hand, giving it a little extra squeeze as he cast his gaze across her opulent bosom.

The general exchanged a few more pleasantries with Longarm and Billy Vail, then, tipping his hat, hooking his arm, and swinging his walking cane, set off through the crowd with his beautiful, black-haired niece in tow. Drifting away, he announced that he had to hail the girl a cab, as his wife was expecting her home for a tea party while the general was heading off for a meeting and poker game with his business associates. When they were ten yards away, Cynthia glanced back over her shoulder, giving Longarm a hurt, smoky look. Then she turned ahead and disappeared with her tall, lordlike uncle into the throngs of milling revelers.

Longarm took a long, frustrated pull off his cigar, then turned to Billy, exhaling a thick smoke plume just above his boss's hatted head. "Billy, you know damn good and well you've had me scheduled for nothing but court duty for the next two weeks!"

The chief marshal chuckled with self-satisfaction but said, "Now, that ain't entirely true. I've been mulling over this rustling up north, and I hadn't quite decided if I wanted to send Ralph White up to check it out, or you. So happens I got a wild hair a moment ago, and decided to send you."

He chuckled again. His pale, clean-shaven cheeks, which had started turning to suet the moment he'd retired his own gun and saddle for an office with his name in gold-leaf letters on the door, quivered and turned pink with self-satisfied glee. He poked his fingers into his pockets and rose again on the toes of his scuffed brogans.

As Longarm opened his mouth to speak, the shorter man wheeled and poked a stubby finger in his face. "And you oughta be thankin' me instead of lookin' like you wanna poke your double-action .44 up my ass and blow a hole through my liver. You been fuckin' that girl seven ways from sundown for nigh on a year now, and sooner or later the general's gonna find out. If he don't shotgun ya, which he *ought* to do, he'll use his influence to get your ass fired!"

"We're very discreet."

"If you're so discreet, how come I know about it?"

"Ah, shit, Billy!" Longarm's eyes grew wide as something dawned on him. He dropped his cigar on the gravel and snapped his fingers. "The old geezer said he was gonna hail her a hack, didn't he?"

Billy scowled, puffing up his carplike face. "Custis, whatever the hell you got on your fool mind now, forget it. That's an order!"

"Best place to hail a hack is at the corner of Cherokee and Mount Evans." Longarm patted his boss's shoulder as he stared off in the direction the general and Cynthia had gone. He turned and began walking backward through the crowd. "I'll see ya tomorrow, Billy."

"Damn your eyes, Long! I just gave you a direct order."

"I ain't on duty, Billy!"

"If you get yourself shotgunned by Denver's founding

father his ownself, who the hell am I gonna assign to the really *tough stuff*?"

But Longarm had already disappeared, running and weaving through the crowd, with only God-knows-what brand of depravity on his mind.

Chapter 3

Longarm hightailed it fast enough through the Fourth of July throng so that, crouching behind the crowd gathered around the pushcart of a Mexican kid peddling hot tamales from his steam chest, he spied the general hailing an enclosed hansom cab for his sweet but not-so-chaste niece at the corner of Cherokee Street and Mount Evans Avenue.

The general received a parting peck on his gray-bearded cheek while the opera-hatted cabdriver held the hansom door wide for the girl. Longarm clucked to himself, chuckled like a mischievous schoolboy, then lit cross-country, jogging through alleys, between several business establishments, through a small feedlot, and across a sprawling wagon yard and a residential district, setting a couple of dogs to nipping at the heels of his cavalry boots. He pulled up between a boardinghouse and a two-story Victorian around which a picket fence was being erected by several half-breeds and a couple of Mexicans who apparently found no reason to celebrate the country's birthday. They were being supervised by a fat German shepherd panting in the shade of a sprawling lilac bush. The dog regarded Longarm skeptically, closing his mouth to sniff the air, black nostrils expanding and contracting. Deciding it was too hot to get up and inspect the interloper more closely, the beefy dog turned back to the workers and let his tongue droop once more over his lower canines, head bobbing as he panted.

Longarm had anticipated the driver's route correctly. The cab's two matched steeldusts were clomping smartly up the cobblestone street from his left. Squatting behind a lilac about fifteen feet from the German shepherd, he waited until the cab had passed his position and was slowing for a choppy section of cobbles and chuckholes in front of the Victorian. Pinching his hat brim at a couple of the fence builders regarding him with the same skepticism as the dog, he jogged into the street, leaped onto the jouncing cab's wooden step, twisted the brass handle forged into the shape of a maple leaf, and drew the door wide.

The possibility that the cab was occupied by someone besides Miss Larimer had been a vague, haunting dread. A quick sweep of the hack's leather-upholstered, velvet-curtained interior put him at ease. Cynthia sat alone in the cab's far corner, riding backward, regarding him lustily from the hansom's deep shadows, one eyebrow arched knowingly.

She put a finger to her deep-dimpled cheek and squinted one almond-shaped eye. "Something told me I might be sharing this fare."

"Damn." Longarm stepped inside, swaying from side to side as the driver negotiated the chuckholes, then pulled the door closed and plopped himself down across from the full-lipped beauty. "I hate bein' predictable."

Cynthia had one arm crossed beneath her bosom, pushing her breasts up so that all but the nipples of her round, hard orbs were exposed and on the verge of exploding from their lair. Her legs were crossed, and she gave her right, pointed-toed, calf-leather half boot a sassy toss.

"When we were standing there with Uncle George and your wretched employer, I saw that your trouser snake was all but ready to strike." Still holding one slim finger to her cheek, she dropped her cool, wistful eyes to his crotch. "And I had a feeling—call it a girl's sixth sense— that you might find a way to intercept me."

She lifted her right boot between his knees and gently touched the toe to his lumpy crotch. "And I was right, wasn't I, Custis?"

Longarm groaned as the girl's toe tickled his swollen cock. Instantly, his body temperature rose about twelve degrees. His heart thudded. As he rolled his eyes around, he saw a pair of sheer white stockings and lacy pink underwear lying bunched beneath Cynthia's seat. "Damn," he wheezed as she continued to caress his member with her boot toe. "I am predictable."

Cynthia chuckled. She dropped her foot to the floor, kicked out of her boots, and jerked her light cotton skirt up to her creamy thighs, which many afternoons on horseback had sculpted to a sumptuous shape and texture. She pinched up the material even farther, until the exposed nap between her legs—the same shade of black as her hair and split vertically by delicate pink lips—made it obvious that the underfrillies beneath the leather seat were, indeed, her own.

When she had the dress arranged the way she wanted it, she dropped her bare knees to the floor and began unbuckling Longarm's gun belt. "Give it to me, Custis." Her voice trilled with the cab's rock and sway and her own desperation. "Thanks to your vile employer, we don't have much time, and I've be dreaming about your big, hard rod inside me ever since I got back from London!"

Longarm began to move his hands toward his belt, but Cynthia had removed it more than a few times before and had already slipped the prong from the leather tongue. The belt and holster fell back on the seat behind him. Just as adroitly, she unfastened the fly buttons of his skintight whipcord trousers, shoved her delicate fist through the crowded gap, and wrapped her cool fingers around his cock.

Longarm grunted as lightning bolts of pounding desire shot up from his belly and into his chest, making his heart roll like a ship on a storm-tossed sea. She fished out the object of her affection until it stood, hard and erect as a bung starter, her pale, quivering hand pumping it slowly.

"Jesus," Longarm rasped as the girl sank back against her own seat and continued manipulating his shaft, her eyes squeezed shut, her whole body trembling.

He leaned sideways and pulled the leather shade away from the window. Having gotten to know this end of town well in recent months, he quickly got his bearings. They had about fifteen more minutes before the austere brick and sandstone mansions of Sherman Street began rearing up along the cobblestone road, maybe another five before they pulled up before the castlelike digs of General Larimer's parapetted fortress.

Releasing the shade, Longarm returned his attention to the beautiful, black-haired, pearl-skinned waif who knelt between his legs with his naked, purple-headed cock in her fist, her eyes closed, head lolling back on her narrow shoulders. Cynthia had pulled her corset all the way down to her waist, laying those full, tender breasts bare. As her nipples stood, pebbled and hard as cask plugs, she leaned forward, stuck out her tongue, and rested its hot, wet tip against the end of his shaft.

A hot bubble rose in Longarm's chest and burst at the base of his throat. "Jesus."

"I like to lick it," she said in a little girl's voice.

"I like it when you lick it."

She lowered her head, pasted her hot tongue to his balls, then slowly ran it up the underside of his shaft to the tip. As she did, Longarm squirmed around on his seat and wrapped his fingers over the bench's upholstered edge, sucking shallow breaths. Cynthia swirled her tongue around on the tip of his swollen cock then looked up at him, grinning.

Still using her little-girl voice, she asked, "Do you like it when I suck it, Custis?"

"Life's too short to ask fool questions, girl."

Giggling, Cynthia closed her lips over the end of Longarm's cock. She slid her mouth down as far it would go, gagging a little, then slowly slid it back off. Her lips made a slight popping sound as they slid up and over the bulging, purple head. Planting her thumb over the tip, she smacked her red, moist lips and lifted her eyes to his, smiling sensuously. "Too bad we don't have a full day to frolic in proper quarters, isn't it, Custis?"

"Well, I reckon that kinda depends on what you call proper, Miss Cynthia."

She smiled and began lowering her head once more. Longarm wrapped his hands around her arms, gently lifted her up, and pushed her back against her seat. "Cust-isss," she complained, "I was just starting to have *fun*."

"Proper quarters or not," Longarm said, "it's time we did this proper."

His dong, glistening with the girl's spittle, jutted up between his thighs and out from under his hanging shirt-tails. He slid his butt to the edge of his seat, snaked his arms around Cynthia's waist, then drew her to him slowly. With one hand, he pushed her dress farther up on her waist. With the other, he snugged her tight against him, until his bobbing cock pressed against her snatch.

Cynthia's mouth opened wide, and she sucked a sharp breath. "Oh, Custisss . . ."

"I apologize in advance for my haste," Longarm growled. "But I reckon we have about ten minutes before your tea party starts."

Longarm grabbed her thighs and drew her to him brusquely. His shaft parted her furred lips, slid deep into her hot, wet, expanding and contracting core. She shuddered in his arms, lifting her chin, closing her eyes, and dropping her jaw.

"Apology accepted," she breathed.

Longarm pushed her back until the furred lips of her love nest were about to slip off the end of his cock, then drew her toward him again.

She groaned, grunted, and sighed. "You do that . . . so well, Custis. Uh, gawd!" she exclaimed as he drew her to-ward him so swiftly that the meeting of their hips made a dull slapping sound.

As she ground her heels into the small of his back, Longarm leaned forward and pistoned the girl back and forth on his lap. Starting slowly, he worked into a gradu-ally quickening rhythm, roughly gauging their approach to climax by the mental map in his head and his approxi-mation of the hansom's distance to the girl's uncle's digs on Sherman Street.

He'd visited the neighborhood enough times by now

that he'd memorized most of the hills, turns, and even the trees lining the thoroughfares—which he could see the few times he turned his head from the bouncing girl in front of him to peer around the drawn shades on both sides of the cab.

Cynthia bounded up and down, up and down, her pale, pink-nippled breasts jouncing and swaying above the pulled-down corset. She clamped her hands around Longarm's neck, occasionally running them brusquely through his hair or pulling his ears or swiping them across his broad, muscular shoulders.

"Oh!" she groaned, keeping her voice low enough that Longarm didn't think the driver could hear. "Oh, yes. Jesus God, yes . . . yesssss . . . uhhh . . . ohhhhhh . . . *yessssssss*!"

With the small part of his brain acting as navigator, Longarm figured they were about to turn into the Larimers' long, climbing, circular drive. If he was correct, they had about three minutes until the hansom pulled up in front of the mansion's front door.

He pushed the girl farther back on her seat and, half-standing and snaking his hands beneath her thighs, pulled her hips up toward him. At the same time, he drove his own hips down and forward, increasing his speed until he was fairly pummeling the girl with his rock-hard organ.

She groaned and sighed and panted and sighed and groaned as Longarm drove himself against her, back and forth, back and forth, his cock like the drive rod on a Baldwin locomotive. Wet slapping sounds rose, and the hansom swayed from side to side on its leather thorough-braces, squawking and creaking. Longarm no longer cared if the driver heard. Hell, he didn't care if the general himself heard.

Lying back against the bench, her head bent uncomfortably against the seat back, Cynthia threw her arms out to both sides and flopped around like a rag doll, her black hair tumbling about her ivory cheeks. Her love moans leaped to shrieks as she and Longarm rose to the very edge of climax.

The pitching wagon slowed.

Longarm gripped the girl's thighs ever harder.

Gritting his teeth, he pulled nearly all the way out of the girl's boiling tunnel before, as the carriage rocked to a stop, he plunged forward once more. He held steadily against her and inside her as his seed fired out the end of his cock like .45 shells from the maw of a finely tuned Gatling gun.

Cynthia began to shriek as though she were being tortured by bronco Apaches. Longarm, shuddering as he emptied his loins inside her, clamped his hand over her mouth, keeping the scream to the pitch and volume of a dreaming cat's.

When he'd fired his last shots, he dropped her thighs and sagged against her, both of them breathing and sweating as though they'd run up a steep hill with demons on their heels.

After the commotion, the silence inside the cab was absolute.

A door opened with a muffled chuff and hinge squawk. An old woman's voice, hesitant, vaguely incredulous, said, "Cynthia, dear?"

Cynthia's eyes snapped wide with shock as she stared up at Longarm sagging atop her. "Aunt Fannie!" she rasped. Then, turning her head toward the hansom's door, she cleared her throat as if to steady her voice, and said sweetly, "Be right out, Auntie—I'm just freshening up a tad!"

"Do hurry, my sweet," Mrs. Larimer said, vaguely admonishing. "The ladies are waiting in the tea parlor. I told them you'd play some Chopin!"

Longarm sagged back in his seat, still breathless, and reached down to pull up his pants. He sat as far back as he could so old Mrs. Larimer wouldn't spot him around the gently buffeting shade. At the same time, Cynthia, who was still trying to catch her own breath, frantically lifted her bodice up over her breasts, dropped her skirts down over her knees, and reached up to pin her hair atop her head. That done, she scooped her feathered hat off the floor, pinned the hat to her hair, and leaned forward to give Longarm a good-bye peck.

"Thanks for the escort, Custis," she said, holding his big face in her hands and smiling devilishly. "Next time I'm in town . . ."

"Wait," Longarm said, plucking a handkerchief from the inside of his coat pocket.

"Cynthia, what on earth is taking so long?" asked the old woman, no doubt still standing in the mansion's open doorway at the top of marble steps abutted on both sides by lounging stone panthers. "Your bags were sent ahead from the train station . . ."

Longarm held the girl's chin in one hand while he gently swabbed sweat from her cheeks with the other.

"There," he said, stuffing the handkerchief back in his pocket.

Cynthia pecked him once more and left, quickly closing the hansom's door behind her as Longarm sank back in the shadows. He listened as she climbed the steps and greeted her aunt in the doorway. When the door closed, muffling the continued conversation, Longarm sank farther back in his seat, sighed, and crossed his legs.

A dry, bemused voice rose from the driver's boot up and forward. "Home, Deputy?"

Longarm chuckled. "Larimer Street, Milt."

The driver clucked to the horses. As the cab pulled ahead, the wheels churning the driveway's deep gravel, Longarm sank bank in his seat like a lord and fished a cheroot from his shirt pocket. "Make it snappy, will you, Milt?" He chewed off the end of the cheroot and spat it on the floor. "I've worked up one hell of an appetite!"

Chapter 4

Longarm wasn't sure if he was being punished for diddling General Larimer's famous niece or if Billy Vail had intended to send him to Snakehead Gap in the desolate wastes of eastern Colorado all along. Maybe Billy didn't really know, himself.

All Longarm knew was that after three blistering hot days of damn hard horseback riding straight west of Denver, he found himself, clad in field denims and a dark-blue work shirt, bellied up against a sage-stippled knoll, adjusting a pair of field glasses and trying to figure out who the hell was on his backtrail.

Holding the glasses down low in the bunchgrass to keep the sun from reflecting off the lenses, he slid his gaze slowly from left to right and then back again.

Nothing out there now but barren, chalky hogbacks tufted here and there with bunchgrass clumps, sage, and Spanish bayonet. A few forlorn cottonwoods or box elder drooped in low areas, stock-still in the unmoving, hot, dry prairie air. A large jackrabbit bounced out from behind a sage tuft about a hundred yards away and disappeared in the sun-bleached rocks hunkered around a knoll.

The rabbit was the only thing that had moved since Longarm had ground tied his horse down in the draw behind him and begun scrutinizing the country he'd just traveled. Off and on since leaving the ramshackle trading post–hotel in which he'd spent the previous night, he'd spied three mare's tails of dust rising behind him, always about a mile off.

Well, hell, he thought, lowering the binoculars. Maybe the riders were cowpunchers who had merely been following the same wagon trail he'd been following and had pulled off toward one of the little shotgun ranches scattered about this hellish country like a handful of dominoes dropped on a vast, wrinkled rug.

He didn't think so, though. He'd been at this business long enough, and had been bushwhacked enough times, to sense when men of dark intent and bitter purpose were fogging his trail.

Rising and brushing the orange dust and weed seeds from his field-grade denims, he cast a cautious glance around. Finding no near signs of an imminent ambush, he tramped off down the draw to where the stout buckskin he'd requisitioned from the federal stables stood nibbling the leaves off a cottonwood sapling, swishing its tail at flies.

He cased his field glasses, dropped them into his saddlebags, and swung up into the saddle, booting the deep-bottomed beast toward the little town nestled between two rocky ridges in the eastern middle distance.

Snakehead Gap.

According to Billy Vail, some crazy regulator named "Loony Larry" Dixon was holed up somewhere around the town, allegedly rustling cows and shooting folks, including the sheriff and deputy sheriff of Snakehead Gap. Loony Larry was a federal problem not only because he'd busted out of federal prison in Montana six months ago, where he'd been locked up for murder and sundry other major and minor offenses, but because he'd killed the two local lawmen, as well.

Longarm's orders were to ride in, throw a loop over Loony Larry, sort out the rustling or land-grab trouble he's involved in, and haul his heinous ass to Denver for transport back to Deer Lodge, Montana Territory, and no doubt a waiting gallows.

"That's some hellish country out there, Custis," Billy had laughed around the stogie in his teeth. "The few scraps of shade are taken up by the rattlesnakes. Hotter'n hell's backside! And, since Snakehead Gap has been without benefit of law for the past three weeks, no telling what kind of vermin you'll find in them dusty, wind-blown streets."

As Longarm had hefted his rifle, bedroll, saddle, and war bag and headed out, Billy's voice had thundered behind him, "I sure hope she was worth it!"

Now Longarm booted the buckskin up out of the draw and onto the well-traveled trail, heading for the motley collection of unpainted wood-frame and adobe buildings, stock pens, corrals, and privies rising out of the orange dust and sage before him. According to the reports Longarm had perused by his first night's campfire, Snakehead Gap had been an old hide-hunter's camp that had grown gradually into a town despite having been burnt twice by rampaging Kiowa and Southern Cheyenne. A few hardy ranchers and farmers had filed on claims along the main creek, the Hatchet Woman, and its four or five tributaries north and east of the town.

As Longarm began cleaving the town's main drag, casting his gaze from the rolling hills and chalky buttes to the

35

run-down, tumbleweed-littered boardwalks around him, he scratched the back of his head and muttered, "Shit, and I thought West Texas was hell with the fires out."

He didn't regret his time between Cynthia's spread legs, however. This town he'd forget as soon as he'd thrown the shackles on Loony Larry Dixon. He'd remember Cynthia on his deathbed.

It was three o'clock on a weekday afternoon, but there weren't more than half a dozen horses tied to hitch racks on either side of the wide, deep-rutted street, most in front of saloons. A tall man with a high-crowned Boss-model Stetson, drooping mustache, and scraggly goatee stood behind the batwings of one mud-brick watering hole, resting his arms on the doors as he stared out from beneath the overhanging brush arbor. A hard, skeptical glint shone in his deep-set brown eyes. Behind him, someone was trying to play a piano while a girl sang almost too softly to hear.

As he passed, Longarm tipped his hat to the man. The gent turned his head to follow Longarm up the street, but made no move to return the gesture.

"Friendly cuss," Longarm muttered. But after hearing the town had been without a sheriff for three weeks, he'd expected to ride into pistol fire and bloody street brawls.

As the buckskin clomped on down the dusty trace, Longarm took note of a squat stone building that the sign in front succinctly identified as the jail. Swinging his head in the opposite direction, he spied another shingle announcing "Vernon C. Wade, Tonsorial and Undertaking Parlor." Vernon Wade, the mayor of this fair city, was Longarm's first contact.

The deputy angled the buckskin to the narrow, two-story, shake-shingled, unpainted building on the left side of the street, before which half a dozen barred rock chickens pecked in the hay- and dung-strewn dust, and drew up before the hitch rack. The coop squatted to the right of the main building, surrounded by chicken wire and shaded by a giant cottonwood. A ladder-backed ramp angled down from the coop's raised front door, strewn with chicken shit and cracked corn. The air around the place was rife with the smell of barn fowl, pomade, tonic water, and the faint, sweet fetor of human remains.

As Longarm swung down from the buckskin and looped the reins over the hitch rack, voices emanated from the shop's open front door, which was flanked by a striped barber pole and a long vertical sign giving hand-scrawled prices for haircuts, shaves, teeth pullings, undertaking services, and caskets. At the bottom, in large red letters, the sign declared "No Credit Given!" Another sign was propped on a bench: "Haircuts May Be Traded For Antelope Thru July."

Longarm stepped into the doorway and squinted into the shadows. A stocky, round-faced gent sat in a barber's chair before several shelves of colored bottles, his bulky frame covered by a washworn sheet. His face was thickly lathered with shaving soap. Another man—a stringbean with close-set eyes, a long hooked nose, and thick, pomaded black hair, stood beside the first, clipping the hair hanging down around the stocky gent's bald pate.

Hearing Longarm's boot squawk a floorboard, both men jerked their startled gazes toward the doorway, their eyes widening slightly as they regarded the dusty, large-framed, mustached gent blocking the light, a Colt .44 positioned for the cross-draw on his left hip.

Longarm's eyes were steel gray as they peered out from beneath the brim of his coffee brown, flat-brimmed

Stetson sitting square on his head and low over his eyes. "The name's Long," Longarm said to the barber. "You Wade?"

The man's eyes shivered in their sockets as they took the big man's measure once more. The stocky gent glanced up at him grimly, his cheeks coloring above the shaving soap. Wade cleared his throat nervously. "Depends on who's askin'."

"Deputy U.S. Marshal Custis Long," Longarm said, hooking his thumbs behind his cartridge belt and leaning a shoulder against the door frame. "First District Court of Denver. I was sent to look into—"

"Oh, Christ, it's the law!" the barber said, dropping his hands to his sides and grinning broadly.

"Whew!" exclaimed the bulky gent in the chair, forming a pink smile inside the snow-white soap. "Are we glad to see you! Word's been gettin' around Snakehead Gap's got no law!"

"Pleased to make your acquaintance, Deputy Long," the barber said, taking his comb and scissors in one hand and pumping Longarm's hand with the other. "I am indeed Vern Wade, barber, undertaker, teeth puller, and mayor of Snakehead Gap. A few folks around here even been trying to get me to pin a badge to my chest, but I say, no sir, I got my hands full here. Besides, I ain't much good with anything but a bird gun!"

"Been havin' trouble, have you?" Longarm said, scratching a match to life and firing the three-for-a-nickel cheroot he'd stuck between his lips. "I mean, besides the fact that both your lawdogs were kicked out with a shovel?"

"Nothing much to speak of just yet. Seen a few pistoleros pull through, sizing up the bank. Though they must've thought it weren't worth the trouble and rode on. Main problem is, knowin' there ain't no badge toters walkin' the streets, even the well-heeled folks tend to get a little too rowdy at night, once they get their tonsils good and greased—if you know what I mean."

The stocky gent said from his chair, "A couple of the saloons been shot up pretty bad by local boys, and a whore got cut a few nights ago."

"She all right?"

"Miss Charlene'll be fine, though her price'll no doubt go down once she's back on her feet. The bastard took a sizable chunk out of her nose."

"Yeah, but she took a sizable chunk out of the john's ass with her pearl-gripped derringer. The man's screams could be heard all over town, settin' babies to wailin' left and right, before his amigos finally got him rode on out of here."

"Hell, it ain't just the whores and waddies lettin' their wolves out," Vernon Wade said. "Mrs. Brindle done laid her husband out so bad with a wash bucket he's still just sittin' on his porch starin' off, sputterin' and mutterin', like his brain's been fried."

"Alvina done caught him frolickin' with the neighbor girl," the stocky gent whispered, holding a hand to his mouth.

"In their wagon shed," added Vernon Wade.

Longarm puffed his stogy and then turned to flick ashes onto the porch where two barred rocks were strutting and pecking at the cracks between the floorboards. "Not to sound bossy or nothin', since I just rode in from the tall and uncut and all, but it appears to me that you and the city council need to put your heads together and come up with another sheriff, Mr. Wade."

"We done tried that," Wade said. "Only no one wants the job. Leastways, not till that hellish Loony Larry Dixon's been rode out of the country. What he did to our two lawdogs has spread like wildfire through this country, and nobody wants the *same* to happen to *them*."

"What'd he do, exactly?"

"Follow me," said Vernon Wade, setting his scissors and comb on a shelf and beckoning to Longarm.

As the man, scrubbing his hands on his striped apron, disappeared through a back door, the bulky gent huffed and puffed as he heaved himself up out of the barber chair. Not bothering to remove the smock bulging across his ample waist or to wipe the shaving soap from his plump cheeks, he quickly shook Longarm's hand, introduced himself as Jack Doyle, harness maker, then scurried back through the same door as Wade.

Longarm puffed the cheroot and glanced out the front door, shuttling his gaze back the way he'd come. He still expected to see the three men who'd been trailing him for most of the day. But there was only a Mexican waddie riding slowly along the other side of the street, a dusty sombrero on his head and a red and white neckerchief flopping around his neck.

As the Mex pulled up before the same cantina in which Longarm had spied the gent with the Boss-model Stetson, the lawman took another deep puff off the cheroot and turned to follow Wade and Doyle through the open door at the back of the barbershop. The door led into a workshop in which caskets in all stages of construction leaned against walls or stretched across sawhorses, tingeing the sickly sweet dead air with the tang of pine.

A large woman with curly red hair stood at a table upon which a skinny cadaver was stretched—a dead man with long black hair hanging over the end of the table, pale blue skin, and pennies over his eyes. The side of his face was a mass of dried blood and purple bruises.

The big redhead, clad in a flour-sack dress and burlap apron, glanced up at Longarm and gave a cordial nod as she lifted a sponge from the wooden bucket beside her, then applied the sponge to the dead man's face.

"Horse threw him," she muttered.

"Olga, that there's the federal badge toter we been waitin' on," said Vernon Wade, flanked by Doyle at the back of the room, near another open door leading outside. "Deputy, that's my wife, Olga. She an' her mother do the cleanin' and dressin', though her mother's took to the sick bed again."

Longarm smiled and pinched his hat brim at the woman. Olga nodded cordially again, then returned to her work, frowning down at the dead man's battered face.

Longarm followed Wade and Doyle out the shop's back door, stepped across a trash-strewn alley, and climbed down a half dozen steps into an adobe-walled, brush-roofed cellar. The place smelled like damp earth and death, and a rat squawked and scuttled across the floor, hidden in the pit's dank shadows.

"I call this my keeper room," Wade said as he moved to where a simple pine coffin stretched across two sawhorses. He grabbed a crowbar and pried the lid off.

The air wafting from the coffin's innards was like sticky fingers sliding down Longarm's throat to tickle his gut. He swallowed quickly to keep from retching, lips stretched back from his teeth.

"Jesus Christ!" exclaimed Jack Doyle, burying his soapy face in his arm.

Wade leaned the coffin lid against the wall, lit a lamp, held it out over the coffin, and glanced at Longarm. "You see that there?"

Swallowing once again and breathing through his mouth, Longarm leaned forward and peered down. Lying in the coffin was a stocky gent—late thirties, early forties—in a checked shirt, leather vest, and canvas pants. He wore no boots, and his left big toe stuck out of its dirty white sock. The man's curly red hair crawled back from a receding hairline, and thick muttonchops of the same color angled down the sides of his gaunt cheeks to form a mustache. There was a small hole in the middle of a broad bloodstain on his upper left chest.

But what caught the brunt of Longarm's attention was the fact that the man's head wasn't connected to his shoulders. It had been cut off, then merely propped at the end of his neck. A jagged, red saw line stretched across his neck, with several grisly gaps showing gristle and liver-colored gore. The man's eyes, receding into their sockets, were wide open and staring, his purple, mustached lips stretched back from his crooked teeth in perpetual agony.

"Christ," Longarm said, drawing on his cigar to kill the cloying fetor in his nostrils. "What the hell happened to him?"

Vernon Wade said, "This here's Randall Grover, hired man out at Ed Tate's North Fork Ranch. Ed woke up one morning last week, slipped out of his cabin to fetch wood for his breakfast fire, and was surprised to find Grover's work wagon sitting in front of the bunkhouse, still hitched to a horse. Randall had gone off to repair fence around Tate's range, and Tate had expected him to be gone all week.

"So, Ed walks out to see what's what, and lo and behold,

look what he finds in the back of the work wagon." The mayor–undertaker nodded at the mutilated corpse before him. "Grover was sitting up against the box, like he was taking a nap. Only his head wasn't where it was supposed to be. He was cradling it in his lap!"

"Ay, yi, yi!" intoned Jack Doyle, his voice muffled as he rubbed his face in his arm.

Billy's report, which included details from Wade's letter to him about the recent killings around Snakehead Gap, had mentioned nothing about decapitations. "This how the lawmen were found?" Longarm asked.

Wade nodded. "Only they were both shot with barn blasters first. Their bodies were tied over their horses' backs and sent home with their heads stuffed in their saddlebags."

"How come you didn't tell that to Marshal Vail?"

"It took me long enough to write what I did," the undertaker said, retrieving the coffin lid from the wall with a grunt. "I ain't exactly the readin' and writin' sort." He set the lid atop the coffin and hammered it closed with the heels of his hands.

"The evil doin's of Loony Larry Dixon, sure enough!" exclaimed Jack Doyle into his arm.

Chapter 5

Being familiar with the smell of death and being accustomed to it were two different things. So when Vernon Wade suggested that he, Longarm, and Jack Doyle return to the barbershop to discuss the situation in less whiffy environs, Longarm agreed.

The lawman sat in a scroll-back chair against the barbershop wall, puffing his stogy, while Wade continued barbering Doyle and filling in the rest of the gaps he'd left out of his letter to Billy Vail—the main one being that some folks in the area believed that Loony Larry Dixon was working for Howard Diamond out at the Diamond Bar B ranch on the East Fork of Hatchet Woman Creek.

"No one knows for sure?" Longarm asked.

Vernon Wade shook his head while he finished cutting Doyle's few remaining strands of gray blond hair. He sharpened a bone-handled razor on the strap hanging down the side of the barber chair.

"No one's actually seen Dixon on Diamond's land, but word has sort of spread around from waddies working the ranches in the area, including a few of Diamond's own men, that Dixon's riding for the Diamond brand. Now, I for one find it hard to believe. Howard Diamond just ain't the sort to hire a regulator, much less a crazy, cockeyed son of a bitch like Loony Larry Dixon!"

"But it's men from the ranches and farms *around* Diamond that have ended up dead and headless," Jack Doyle pointed out, slitting a look at Longarm. "And none of them boys have the money to hire a regulator, or the need. Hell, they're all tiny outfits, shotgun ranches and dirt farms. They have a hard enough time feedin' their whelps. There wouldn't be nothin' left over for hirin' a regulator, even if they had the need for one."

"Why do you say Diamond ain't the sort to hire a killer?" Longarm asked, glancing at one of the barred rocks poking its curious head in the barbershop door.

Wade shrugged. "Howard's a God-fearin' man. He was the first to settle this country and start the town. He always welcomed new folks, saying 'the more the merrier' and 'there's wealth in numbers.' A greedy man Howard was not."

The barber stopped the razor's slide across Doyle's cheek, frowning pensively at the soap bunched up in front of the blade. "Of course, I ain't seen ole Howard in a month of Sundays. Ain't seen him in church or the mercantile or his favorite saloon, the Hatchet Woman, for a hell of a long time. Maybe he's gone loco, brush poppin' out there so far from town with only those four crazy girls of his fer company . . ."

Chuckling dryly, Wade continued sliding the razor across Doyle's cheek.

Longarm arched a brow. "Girls?"

"Four of the looniest little bitches you ever seen in your life," Doyle said as Wade started on his other cheek.

Wade stopped and half turned toward Longarm, extending the razor for emphasis, "But pretty as speckled pups, every one! When those little bitches ride to Snakehead Gap for supplies or church or whatnot, they turn the heads of every man in town."

"And make the boys cream their drawers!" Doyle chuckled.

"Ain't just the boys who cream their drawers at the sight of that Miss Aubrey," confessed Vernon Wade, shaking his head. "When I see her in those little flowery dresses with necklines down to her belly button—I damn near forget I'm a happily married man!"

"Aubrey, hell!" Doyle exclaimed. "You ever seen Wanda ride in, wearing those skintight jeans and men's shirts without nothin' underneath? That copper-haired vixen can start a saloon brawl without even walkin' near a saloon!"

"I've heard tell that Cassie used to blow the old schoolmaster for A's, and when he—"

"All right, boys," Longarm interrupted the barber, puffing the cigar and gaining his feet. "I believe we're getting sidetracked. But I probably have as much information as I need to get started trailin' this Loony Larry Dixon . . . except directions out to the Diamond Bar B ranch."

Wade told him to follow the main trail straight east out of town, along the main fork of Hatchet Woman Creek, and continue through a jog of rocky hills. Turn left where the trail forked, about five miles from town. He'd find a sign for the Diamond Bar B under a sprawling cottonwood at the crossroads. It was about a ten-mile ride.

"You gonna just waltz out there and arrest him?" Doyle asked, incredulous.

"Why not?"

"Don't you need proof he done it?"

"Nope," Longarm said, turning to flick his cigar into the street. "The son of a bitch escaped from prison up Montana way. All I have to do is arrest him. If he's like most hired guns, when I *do* arrest him, he'll probably start shouting the name of the man who hired him at the top of his lungs. Chances are I'll be riding back to town with both Loony Larry and Howard Diamond in shackles and handcuffs—if Diamond's the one who hired him, that is."

"Just can't believe Howard would do such a thing," Jack Doyle said. He and Wade were staring pensively at Longarm. "But who else around here has enough money to hire a *regulator*?"

"He no doubt got greedy," Wade said regretfully. "Got tired of sharing them creeks and water holes with the other small ranchers and farmers crowdin' in around him. He's got them damn girls to feed, and it don't look like any of 'em plan on leavin' home."

"I'll be needin' the key for the jailhouse," Longarm said, holding out his hand.

"It ain't locked," Wade laughed. "Hell, Marshal, no one wants to break *into* a jailhouse, don't ya know? Most folks wanna break *out* of one!"

Wade and Doyle laughed heartily.

"You'll find the keys to the cells in one of Sheriff Longtree's desk drawers," Wade called, still chuckling.

Longarm pinched his hat brim, offered a tolerant smile, then headed outside to his horse. "Small towns," he grumbled as he walked over and plucked his reins from the hitch rack.

He glanced up the street the way he'd come, and frowned. About a block away, three new horses stood tied to a hitch rack before the Hatchet Woman Saloon and

48

Dance Hall. One was slurping water from a stock trough while the other two stood hanging their heads wearily. Sweat lather glistened on their necks, withers, and bellies.

Still frowning, puzzled and wary, Longarm led the buckskin slowly down the street, scrutinizing the three horses while skidding his gaze to the batwings in the saloon's front wall, on either side of plate-glass windows. He stopped a few feet in front of the horses—a rangy piebald, a hammer-headed black mare, and a pinto Shetland pony.

All three horses had been ridden a long ways through the hot afternoon. Were they the ones fogging Longarm's trail?

The deputy marshal looped the buckskin's reins over the hitch rack. Unsnapping the keeper thong from over the hammer of his Colt .44, he stepped quietly onto the boardwalk in front of the saloon and stopped before the batwings. He snaked his right hand across his belly to rest it on the forward-jutting grip of his Colt and peered over the doors and into the misty shadows within.

The bar ran along the room's right side. The aproned bartender was turned to the back bar, washing glasses. A dozen round tables were scattered between the bar and the saloon's left wall. Only one of the tables was occupied— by three men in dusty, sweat-stained trail garb.

One sat flipping through a newspaper while he nursed a beer. Another was slumped forward with his head on the table near an empty shot glass and beer schooner. His hat was tipped forward off his head, and he was sending up snores like summer thunder.

The third man sat with his back to Longarm. Only he wasn't a man but a boy, the deputy discovered as he saw the little red black-stitched cowboy boots hanging nearly a whole foot above the floor. The kid wore a brown leather vest and twill trousers shoved into his boots, with a little straw hat perched upon his little head, a red hawk's feather jutting up from the snakeskin band. Judging by his size, the lad was about seven or eight. He appeared to be laying out a game of solitaire on the table before him, taking his time, carefully pondering his cards before setting them down with resolute snaps.

One of the other men at the table was probably the kid's father. He'd taken the boy and his hired man to town to kick up their heels a little before heading back to their shotgun ranch with fresh food for the larder. They hadn't been following Longarm at all. They'd just been taking the same trail as he'd been taking, probably dropping back now and then to let the lad and his little Shetland pony have a rest.

Relieved, Longarm turned around and plucked the buckskin's reins from the hitch rack. He backed the horse once more into the street and shuttled his gaze left and right, looking for a hotel.

He'd have stayed in the jailhouse, but until he had Loony Larry in hand, he didn't want word spreading that a federal badge toter was in the area. He wanted first drop on the kill-crazy hombre. Longarm would keep his head low tonight and head out to the Diamond Bar B first thing in the morning.

After a short scout around the town, he spied a three-story, adobe brick hotel sitting along a side street, well off the town's beaten path. He went over and rented a room, signing himself in as Calvin Lonnigan and leaving the "occupation" column blank. From his dress, most folks would take him for a drifting cowpuncher.

When he'd stowed his gear in his room, he stabled the buckskin in the livery barn next door, owned by the same gent who owned the hotel. Both were tidy, humble outfits without much business at the moment—a good place for hanging low and getting a good night's rest after three days on the hot trail from Denver.

The hotel had a small dining room, so Longarm didn't have to leave the premises for supper—chewy pot roast with canned greens and mashed potatoes and a glass of frothy buttermilk. He followed the meal up with a couple shots of rye in his room, and turned in nearly as early as he'd turned in after his frolic with Cynthia Larimer.

He woke up in the middle of the night, the pot roast and milk mewling and groaning in his gut, and took the hotel's rear outside stairs to the two-hole privy in the back yard. Finished with his business, he'd just straightened to pull up his underwear when the faint crunch of a footstep sounded in the quiet night outside the privy.

His underwear only half raised, he jerked his head up to peer out through the cracks between the door's vertical planks. Above the hotel, a powder horn moon, veiled by high, thin clouds, shed a ghostly light over the hotel and into the yard around the privy. The hotel's back wall and the two stacks of firewood abutting it were in deep shadow.

Nothing moved except for the leaves of the cottonwood to the right of the privy. No sounds except for the slight rustle of the branches.

Figuring what he'd heard had just been a tumbleweed or a cat, he finished pulling up his drawers. Jerking his hat down low on his forehead, he reached for the door's locking nail.

Again there rose the soft, muffled crunch of a foot

coming down on dry grass and coarse gravel. Longarm stayed his hand, shoved his hat brim off his forehead, and crouched to peer once more between the door planks.

Near the hotel's left corner, a shadow moved. Against the hotel's inky silhouette, the shadow was merely a vague shift of black on black, and it seemed to be fairly low to the ground—maybe a dog or a wolf prowling around town, sniffing for scraps. Figuring he'd best take no chances, he reached for his Colt, cursed when his hand found only his hip sheathed in his thin, threadbare underwear shorts.

He usually wore his gun to the privy, but he'd been so groggy that he'd settled for just his hat.

Outside, the small figure continued to move against the hotel's back wall. There was a thump, as of a boot kicking a log, and the rasp of a breath drawn in fury. For a moment the shadow stopped, and Longarm lost track of it until it began moving again, taking shape and definition as it moved out away from the hotel toward the privy.

It stepped out from the hotel's shadow, and moonlight washed over a small hat with a curled brim and a feather protruding high above the crown. Beneath the hat was a face still cloaked in shadow, and a small, oddly shaped body no larger than a seven- or eight-year-old boy's. The boy was crouched, holding something straight out in front of his chest.

Longarm could hear the soft footsteps more clearly now—the crunch of grinding gravel and of occasional snapping weed stems. The kid was breathing regularly but deeply, the air rattling in his nostrils.

As the little hatted figure drew within twenty yards of the privy, moonlight fell across iron. And then the double-barreled, sawed-off shotgun in the kid's hands was clearly etched by the silver light, and Longarm's gut twisted and his heart turned a somersault.

"Shit," he breathed, one eye peering out the crack between the planks.

He looked around quickly. Most privies didn't have back doors, and to Longarm's discontent, this one was no exception. It also had a solid roof. Feeling the walls and the roof closing around him, Longarm said tightly through the crack, "I don't know who said you could play with grownup guns, sonny, but—"

Bizarre, raucous laughter cut him off. "Die, you big son of a bitch! *DIE!*"

Longarm threw himself right as both bores of the sawed-off barn blaster exploded at once, the ear-shattering detonation making the whole privy jump. Longarm hit the floor in front of the two-seater's second hole, slamming his head and jamming his left shoulder against the far wall.

Behind him, two wads of steel buckshot slammed through the door, carving a pumpkin-sized gap in both the door and the back wall above the hole. Wood chunks and slivers flew in every direction. The wall jammed against Longarm's head and shoulder shuddered as though a freight train were hammering toward it.

Outside the privy, the kid—or whatever the shotgun-wielding beast was—roared with maniacal laughter.

Ears still ringing, Longarm heaved himself to his feet, and pushing off the walls around him, staggered to what remained of the door and burst through it. He bolted straight out into the yard, the remaining slats and chunks of the door flying out around him.

As he flew, he saw the pint-sized, feather-hatted silhouette jerk with a start, crouching over his breached

53

barn blaster and looking up, shocked. Before the little beast could dodge, Longarm had him on the ground, squirming around beneath him and cursing like a Norwegian sailor on New Year's Eve in Paris, France.

"Get the fuck off me, goddamn ye! Get the hell off me, ya big son of a ten-cent San Francisco whore!"

The kid or whatever was quick and slippery, and before Longarm knew it, he'd wriggled out from under Longarm and was gaining one of his red-stitched, little-boy boots. Longarm rolled onto a shoulder and grabbed the boot as the little beast bolted forward.

"Ach!" the beast cried as he hit the ground on his belly.

A pistol barked in the darkness somewhere behind Longarm. He flinched as the bullet spanged off a rock six inches from his right hand. Running footsteps and enervated breaths rose on both sides—two men hoofing it toward him and the cursing, grunting beast on the ground before him.

Another pistol shot rang out, this time from Longarm's left. The slug sizzled over Longarm's head and smashed into the hotel's back wall with a sharp thwack. Longarm had seen a six-shooter holstered on the little gent's left hip. Holding the boot with one hand, his heart racing and ears still ringing, Longarm reached for it, wrapped his fingers around the bone grip, and slipped the iron from the leather sheath.

"Give me that, you bastard!" the beast shouted, flailing at Longarm with his tiny, knobby hands.

Longarm brought his right arm back and forward, smashing the back of his hand and the pistol butt against the little beast's cheek. The beast groaned as he twisted around on his hips and dropped to his belly, growling like a wounded bobcat.

Longarm pushed up on his butt to see two tall figures moving toward him, one from the privy's left side, the other from the right, pistols raised. One man's gun flashed. As the bullet plunked into the ground in front of the lawman, spraying dirt and grit over him and the beast, Longarm aimed the Schofield and fired.

The man on the left sucked a sharp breath and dropped to his knees.

The echo of Longarm's first shot hadn't died before he swung right and fired again. The other shooter jerked around with a yowl and triggered his own revolver into the ground at his feet. He howled again, hopped on one foot, loosed a shrill curse, then ran limping back the way he'd come.

On one hip, Longarm turned back to the first shooter. The man lay slumped over his knees as though in some Middle Eastern prayer. He wasn't moving.

"Ohhhhhh," the beast moaned, clawing at the ground with his hands.

Longarm looked around to make sure no one else was drawing a bead on him, then pushed to his knees, grimacing at the thorns chewing through his longhandles and his bare feet. He grabbed the beast's right arm and heaved him over. Longarm guessed he weighed about eighty pounds. He wasn't much over four feet long, with a stout chest, potbelly, and short, bowed legs.

This was no kid. This was a dwarf. What Longarm could see of the man's face in the moonlight—deep-set eyes next to a bulbous nose, and alligator-like skin drawn taut over broad cheeks and a lantern jaw, with a fringe of stubble resembling hog hair—rocked the lawman back on his haunches.

He could almost smell the incense and hear the incantations of some weird, forbidden magic flinging hexes this way and that around him. He stared down at this squirming, mewling ghost from his past, his heart tattooing against his ribs.

"Goddamnit, I already killed you, you little fucker!"

Chapter 6

"You killed my *twin brother*, ya cow-ugly, dung-eatin', privy snipe!" The dwarf lifted his head and spat hot saliva on Longarm's cheek, his beer-sour breath wafting. "The only brother I had—the only kin I had in all the world—and *you* killed him!"

Longarm sleeved the hot, vile goo off his cheek and, despite having been nearly cut in two while sitting over a privy hole with his drawers pulled down around his ankles, he knew a moment's relief. The evil dwarf who'd crucified the mayor of Chugwater, Wyoming, in the buttes overlooking the town, and who'd held the town in a stranglehold of illegal taxes and crooked gambling, had not somehow risen from his wormy grave, after all.

This was his brother.

On his knees and aiming the dwarf's own revolver at the vile creature's hedgehog face, Longarm said, "You're . . . ?" He couldn't remember the other dwarf's name. This repellant creature's equally repulsive twin was called only "The Dwarf," as Longarm recalled.

"I'm Tim Turley," spat the dwarf before Longarm, "Titus's twin brother, you murderin' fuck!"

"Ah, Titus Turley," Longarm said. "Shit on a shingle—my frail faith has done been pinched even thinner. How in the hell could an abomination like that have a *twin*?"

"You killed him!" Tim Turley snarled, holding his bloody cheek with one hand while kicking his little boots and snarling up at Longarm. "You killed my only livin' kin, and I was gonna gun ya in your bed. But when I seen you head out to the privy, I got an even better idea!"

"I didn't kill your brother, Turley," Longarm said. He'd merely escorted an eyewitness to the dwarf's murdering of the Chugwater mayor to Turley's trial. "But I did make sure the little bastard swung!"

He stood, grabbed the dwarf's arm, and jerked him to his feet. The dwarf turned to him, wide-eyed, thin hair swirling around the top of his nearly bald, hatless head. Longarm aimed the cocked revolver at Turley's face and the dwarf stumbled backward, his ugly features blanching as he raised his hands, palms out.

"Oh, Lord, don't shoot me!"

"What in the hell led you to my trail, you dry-gulchin' little fuck?"

The dwarf's large, deep-set eyes jerked to where the dead man lay and in the direction the other one had run. "Sandy and Stretch seen ya at the roadhouse last night. They rode out and picked me up at the line shack."

Longarm looked the dwarf up and down, incredulous. "You ride for a brand?"

"I *cook*!" the little man squealed, jutting his head forward. "And I cook *good*, too."

58

"Well, let's see how well you cook in the federal pen." Longarm glanced around to make sure the bushwhacker he'd wounded hadn't returned, then jerked the little man around by his arm and rammed the gun into his back, prodding him forward through the gap between the hotel and the livery barn.

He hadn't figured on any prisoners besides Loony Larry himself and possibly the man who'd hired him, but he wasn't going to turn Tim Turley loose to try dry-gulching him again. He'd turn the key on the other man, too, if he found him, but he had a feeling the dwarf's accomplice was hobbling back to where he'd come from.

When Longarm and the dwarf were halfway down the gap, Longarm walking tenderly on his bare feet and wincing at the nips of sharp gravel and goatheads, a light appeared ahead. It seemed to float suspended in the air by itself until Longarm drew within twenty yards and saw the silhouette of a black-haired man in a ratty white sleeping shirt and slippers.

"Good Lord," Vernon Wade complained. "What in the hell is goin' on *now*?"

"This little shit tried to ventilate me."

Wade lowered the lamp and turned his head this way and that as he scrutinized the dwarf. "Who the hell's *he*?"

"Your worst fuckin' nightmare, saphead!" the dwarf barked, rising up on the balls of his little boots to glare into the mayor–undertaker's face.

"It runs in the family," Longarm told Wade. Then he asked the mayor to hold the gun on the little polecat while he, Longarm, retrieved his own gun and boots so he could haul the dwarf over to the prison and turn the key on him.

"What if he tries to run?" Wade said, holding the dwarf's Schofield in one hand, the lamp in the other.

"Shoot him," Longarm said, mounting the hotel's front porch.

Longarm didn't bother dressing, as it was still relatively warm and, it being two o'clock in the morning, the streets would be deserted. He just wrapped his Colt and cartridge belt around his lean hips, donned his socks and boots, grabbed a cheroot, and went back downstairs.

The hotel proprietor, a squat, gray-haired man named Wilfred Ramsay, was peering out a window facing the gap between the hotel and the livery barn. "What's going on out there, sir?" he asked, keeping his voice low, though Longarm hadn't seen another boarder. "Had you taken part in all that shooting?"

"I reckon I had at that, Mr. Ramsay," Longarm said, scraping a match to life on the desk as he headed for the front door. "But all's well now. You can go on back to bed."

"I had a feeling you'd be trouble!" the old man rasped, shaking a crooked finger as Longarm, pausing to touch fire to his cigar, went on out the door.

"This is one vile creature," Wade said, turning as Longarm approached the mayor–undertaker and the dwarf. "You should have heard the language he's been using to castigate me, just because I wouldn't accept two silver eagles to turn over his gun!"

"Yellow-bellied squaw fucker!" the dwarf hissed, snakelike, rising up on the balls of his feet to glare up from beneath the gun angled toward his toadlike face. "Does your pig mother know you fuck little Injun girls and dead dogs?" The dwarf squealed a laugh, pleased with himself.

Vernon Wade shook his head and turned again to Longarm, hang-jawed. "Who'd have thought a pint-sized little twerp like this could hold so much bile! Normally I feel sorry for the little folks, as they can't help how they was born. But if you wanted to shoot this thimble-sized demon seed, Deputy, I'd help you scratch a hole for him in the ravine out yonder. Mum's the word, and hell, who'd miss this little pile of green dog shit, anyways?"

"Your wife would, that's who!" the dwarf barked, lifting a leg to slap his thigh, then throwing his head back on his shoulders, cackling like a warlock.

"Don't tempt me, Mr. Wade," Longarm said, taking the dwarf's six-shooter from the man. He was amazed at how closely the dwarf favored his dead twin—in both looks and temperament. "The jail's open, you say?"

"Yeah, it's open. I'll walk over there with you, as it's on my way. My offer's still good, if you change your mind between here and there."

Longarm and Wade walked the dwarf through the dark, moonlit streets, stoically enduring the beast's incessant, vulgar tirade against themselves and their families several generations back. Longarm told Wade to keep an eye on the jailhouse while he was off on Loony Larry's trail, and to feed the little bastard. He was stumped for a response when, staring in horror at the little creature dancing around before them still spewing verbal filth, the mayor–undertaker asked him why'd want to keep such a foul furnace stoked.

When Longarm had locked the dwarf in a cell of the crude but tight, earthen-floored jailhouse, he turned the cell key over to Wade, who then headed back to his shop across the street, swinging his lantern down low beside his flapping nightshirt. Longarm closed the jailhouse door on Tim Turley's tireless tirade and tramped back to the hotel, where he managed to catch three more hours of shut-eye before the roosters and songbirds woke him at first light.

He downed a quick but rib-sticking breakfast, saddled the buckskin, and rode north out of town along Hatchet Woman Creek as the sun blossomed like a giant marigold above the low, sage-covered hogbacks rolling out before him like the swells of a vast ocean. The day heated up quickly, and he wasn't far from town when he shrugged out of his denim jacket and tied it to his blanket roll.

Following Vernon Wade's directions, he rode along the main branch of the creek for about five miles. The crossroads appeared before him, and on the other side of the cross trail a tall, sprawling cottonwood stood, its green leaves flashing golden in the mid-morning sunlight. Below the tree stood a crude wooden sign with the words "Diamond Bar B Ranch." A newer, less weathered sign stood to the right of the first, saying, "No Trespassing. This Means You!"

Something hung from a stout branch. As Longarm heeled the buckskin closer, he found himself staring up at a hang rope dangling there beneath the branch, swaying gently in the warm breeze. The noose dangled level with Longarm's head. Scrutinizing the rope, he saw that the bottom of the noose was flecked with dried, brown blood and bits of dried skin.

Longarm looked around, feeling a slight hitch in his neck and absently fingering his .44's grip. If the noose was a warning about venturing onto Diamond land, it didn't appear to be backed up with armed men sitting on the surrounding ridge crests.

Longarm drew the .44 higher on his left hip and gigged the claybank through the cottonwood's shade and north along the trail, casting his cautious gaze along the ridges and boulders surrounding him. To his right, the north fork of Hatchet Woman Creek trickled in a deep bed. When he'd ridden a mile onto Diamond range, he turned the horse into the ravine and let it drink at the narrow stream fetid with the smell of midsummer water.

Deciding to let the horse have a breather, he loosened its saddle cinch, slipped its bit, then sat on a shaded, deadfall cottonwood for a quick smoke. He hadn't gotten the cheroot out of his shirt pocket, however, before a pistol cracked somewhere on the other side of the creek.

He stared at the buttes rising above the stream's far bank—several large, eroded camelbacks tufted with spindly brown brush clumps and Spanish bayonet. Beyond them, more revolvers popped and the thunder of galloping horses rose. Dust lifted in a crease between two of the buttes to Longarm's left, and then a rider appeared, galloping hard. It was a woman in black pants, boots, and a vest. Her tan arms were bare, and long, thick, copper-colored hair bounced across her shoulders as the horse dropped down an incline, heading toward the creek.

As the horse followed a path down the side of the ravine, about fifty yards upstream from Longarm, several more riders appeared in the gap the girl had just ridden through—five men, whooping and hollering and triggering revolvers, smoke puffing around their hats. They plunged down the incline as the girl, galloping hell-for-leather atop a long-legged steeldust, splashed across the stream and bounded up the bank to Longarm's right, disappearing behind him.

As the five men plunged down the ravine's far bank and into the creek bed, Longarm ran to the nervously prancing buckskin and shucked his Winchester '73 from the saddle boot. Behind him, hooves thudded. The girl had apparently turned to gallop toward him along the trail.

Longarm levered a round into the Winchester's breech and jogged toward the creek bank. On the trail following the lip of the bank, he saw the girl pass in a brown and gray blur between the sprawling cottonwoods. He ran up the bank, breathing hard and gritting his teeth, holding the Winchester in one hand, his low-heeled boots slipping in the fine clay.

When he crested the bank, the girl on the steeldust was galloping out of sight to his right. The five riders were galloping toward him on his left, still whooping and yelling.

Longarm stepped into the middle of the trail and, facing the five riders, fired three quick shots into the air. They all hauled back on their reins at once. All five horses skidded to quick halts in the trail, one of the mounts giving an indignant whinny, the men suddenly falling silent. They stared straight ahead through the billowing dust, eyes snapping wide. They glanced at each other, grumbling warily. Then, as a group, they jerked their horses around without firing a shot.

"Let's get out of here!" the lead rider growled.

They spurred their horses back the way they'd come and disappeared around a bend in the trail.

Hoofbeats sounded behind Longarm. He wheeled quickly, aiming the Winchester as he levered another round. It was the girl, riding back toward him, the steel-dust favoring its right front hoof. The girl had a silver-plated, pearl-gripped revolver in one hand. Its match was holstered in the cross-draw position on her right hip.

As she drew within twenty yards, Longarm's blood warmed.

The face beneath the dusty, man's Stetson was oval-shaped and brown-eyed, with a pert nose and strong jaw and chin. She was perfectly tanned, and her hair, straight as a horse's mane, shone in the sun like freshly minted copper. Above her waist, she wore only a thin, doeskin vest trimmed with hammered silver discs and whang strings. The vest was secured across her breasts with strips of braided rawhide, leaving a good two-inch gap between the flaps. The cleavage was deep and alluring, her arms long and subtly muscled.

She frowned down at him as she drew back on the fiddle-footed steeldust's reins, regarding him with an almost savage intensity. "Who are you?"

Longarm lowered the Winchester's barrel. "Cal Lonnigan." As if of their own accord, his eyes sized her up once more, drinking in her knee-buckling beauty. "Who're you?"

"You're on Diamond Bar B land—you know that, don't you?"

Longarm snorted. "You're welcome."

She glanced in the direction in which her pursuers had vanished. "I would have fought it out with them, but one of my revolvers jammed, and I'm low on ammunition."

"Why were they fogging you?"

"I shot one of 'em in the leg." She stared coolly at Longarm, hiked a shoulder in an offhand manner. "He was on Bar B range, and we've told those squatters many times what would happen if we caught them on our land."

"I saw the message hanging from the cottonwood back at the crossroads."

"It hasn't been as effective as you'd think." She gigged the horse up to Longarm, turned the limping steeldust sideways, and quirked her rich lips in a wry smile. "You rode right past it."

"Just passin' through."

"On the way to where?"

"Anywhere I can find a job."

Her eyes glinted copper as they shunted up and down his tall frame and across his shoulders and chest, the open top buttons of his sweat-damp work shirt exposing several swirls of thick, brown hair.

Her tanned cheeks flushed slightly as she returned her eyes to his. "How 'bout a job giving me a lift home? The steeldust plundered a gopher hole a ways back." She glanced to the east, where the sky was purpling with an oncoming storm. "I don't think there's another mile left in that hock."

Not wanting to look too eager, Longarm didn't say anything, though inwardly he was kicking up his heels. This couldn't be playing out much better. If his luck held, he'd have Loony Larry behind bars by sundown. He canted his head slightly and narrowed an eye with feigned reluctance.

"There'll be a meal in it for you," she said. "And a warm bed."

The corners of Longarm's mouth rose slightly as his eyes dropped to her breasts pushing out the doeskin vest.

"In the bunkhouse," the girl crisply added.

Distant thunder rumbled.

Chuckling and shouldering the Winchester, Longarm headed for the creek and his horse.

Chapter 7

Longarm led his buckskin up to where the girl crouched, examined her steeldust's right front hock, and felt another lust pang as her large breasts bulged out the top of her vest. He realized why Vernon Wade and Jack Doyle had expostulated so long and energetically on the beauty of Howard Diamond's tribe of females.

"Which one are you?"

She straightened, frowning at him curiously.

Longarm hiked a shoulder. "I heard in town that Howard Diamond has a whole stable of daughters, every one pretty as a speckled pup."

"Wanda," she said dryly, not reacting to the compliment. "And you'll still be sleeping in the bunkhouse."

Longarm swung into the saddle with a sigh. "Can't blame me for tryin'." He extended a hand to her. She took it and, holding the steeldust's reins, poked her man's boot in his stirrup and swung up behind him.

As he gigged the buckskin forward, thunder rumbled again, louder this time. The storm front—purple as a ripe plum—was broiling in from the east, turning the buttes on the other side of the creek bed a sickly yellow green.

"Hold on!" Longarm heeled the buckskin into a gallop. Wanda Diamond wrapped her arms around his waist, pressing her breasts against his back and causing fire in all directions from his crotch.

Both horses whinnied and balked as the storm front swooped in, shepherding a cold wind in front of it. As the wind increased and the rain began, Longarm tipped his hat brim low and hunkered over the lunging buckskin's neck. Wanda Diamond slid up even closer, until he could feel the firm warmth of her breasts through his shirt.

Lightning flashed and the rain fell in sheets, instantly turning the trail into a stream.

"We'd best hole up!" Longarm shouted, mud splashing up around his stirrups from the buckskin's pounding hooves.

"There is no place to hole up out here!" the girl said, her voice nearly drowned by the hammering wind and rain and cymbal-like crashes of thunder. "Keep going. We've only a mile or so to go!"

Longarm stretched his gaze out ahead of them. Through the slanting javelins of gray rain, he could see a house towering on a distant, flat-topped butte shouldering back against the purple sky. It was hard to tell from this distance, but it looked like a rambling, mansard-roofed Victorian with jutting brick chimneys and a broad front porch supported by scrolled pillars.

If the house wasn't an illusion somehow manufactured by the weather, it was like something you'd see on Sherman Street in Denver—not out here on this barren, godforsaken prairie.

Longarm lowered his head once more and ground his heels into the buckskin's flanks. The horse splashed around a long bend in the trail and began descending a long, slow incline. About a hundred yards ahead, there was the dark, irregular line of a canyon or ravine running across the trail. As the buckskin continued lunging forward, it became apparent that the gap in the hills had become a white-capped, clay-colored millrace churning with floodwater.

"It's all right," the girl said when she felt Longarm's back tense. "There's a bridge! Keep going!"

Longarm kept the buckskin galloping. The hooves hammered the trail, mud and water splashing up around Longarm and the girl so that several times the lawman had to sleeve the mess from his eyes. The horse bounded up a slight rise at the edge of the ravine, then plunged down the other side.

"On second thought!" the girl screamed. "I haven't seen a rain like this in a long time. The bridge might've been washed out!"

Longarm's gut dropped. His eyes snapped wide and his lower jaw fell. The bank had been chewed away by the flood, and—as the girl had feared—the bridge was gone. But it was too late for Longarm to do anything about it.

The horse screamed as it plunged straight down toward the broiling, tea-colored river.

"We're going in!" he shouted. *"Hold on!"*

The horse screamed again, but the exclamation was clipped as the buckskin's head plunged into the frothy maelstrom. Longarm sucked a sharp breath as the cold water rose up around him, wrapping his entire body instantly in its roaring, icy fingers.

The horse rolled, and Longarm slid off the right stirrup, feeling Wanda's hands grab at his shirt, then slip away. The racing current turned him this way and that, and

71

he saw Wanda's head bobbing above the water about six feet away, her hat floating behind her, the braided thong wrapped around her neck. As they were both swept downstream by the raging current, the buckskin ahead and the steeldust behind, Longarm threw an arm toward the girl. He caught her bare arm in his hand, jerked her toward him, then wrapped his arm around her chest.

Tightening his hold, bringing her against him, he peered downstream. The bank was six feet high on both sides—six feet of slick, fast-eroding mud. There was nothing to grab on to.

The stream was an iron fist, pulling and pushing and churning him downstream. He tipped his head back to draw shallow breaths, but water lapped over his lips and nose and gushed down his throat and into his sinuses.

The rain slanted down in billowing sheets. Witchfingered lightning bolts flashed in the near-black sky. Thunder crashed like tumbling boulders.

Longarm shook his head, coughing, and looked around once more.

The right bank was sloping down. Ahead, approaching quickly, the leafy crown of a recently fallen tree arced over the streambed, about three feet above the water.

"Hold on!" he shouted again as Wanda twisted and turned before him, coughing and flailing her arms desperately.

Longarm kicked right, fighting the current. Ahead, the tree shot toward him, the individual branches and leaves growing larger and larger.

He gritted his teeth as the tree swept within ten yards, then five . . .

"Uhhh!" Longarm grunted as he flung his left arm up. He hooked it over a sodden branch about twice as thick as his arm. The stream and the girl pushed against him. The branch broke with a crack.

The stream heaved them mercilessly forward, snapping several smaller branches, twigs and leaves swatting and scratching Longarm's face. His arm snaked over another branch—a larger, stouter limb.

This one held.

Leaning against the branch, Longarm grunted again and heaved the girl up out of the water, twisting slightly as he flung her up and over the branch. She wrapped her arms around the limb.

"I've got it!" she shouted, lifting a leg.

When she'd gotten both legs on the branch, she crawled away toward the bank. Longarm watched her slender figure fade in the falling rain and sodden leaves, then hoisted himself onto the branch. He crawled forward, grabbing at the branches jutting around him.

Soon the bank appeared on both sides. Longarm had never been so relieved to see solid ground. The girl leaned against the side of the tree, bent forward at the waist, hands on her knees, catching her breath.

When she turned toward Longarm, her vest pulled open, exposing her breasts. The firm, pink-nippled orbs jostled and swayed between the leather flaps of the vest as she reached for him, grabbed his arm, and helped him down off the branch.

His boots slipped in the sodden clay. The girl yowled as they both went down, Longarm landing on his back, the girl belly-down on top of him, her naked breasts flattening against his chest. In spite of his bone-deep damp chill and sore shoulder, a surge of lust ran through him. He wrapped an arm around the girl's shoulders, lifted her chin, drew her even closer, and kissed her.

She returned the kiss, opening her lips for him, pressing her tongue against his. She caressed his chest with her breasts, groaning.

Suddenly, she lifted her head. Lightning flashed, causing her brown eyes to spark as she stared down at him angrily. She lifted her right hand and smashed it hard against his cheek.

Thunder barked almost straight above them, causing the ground to lurch beneath them.

His blood boiling with irresistible passion, Longarm grabbed her hand before she could smack him again. Shoving her hand away, he pulled her head down to his, pressed his lips against hers once more.

She squirmed against him, grunting, fighting him, but then, suddenly, her body relaxed and her lips became supple as the wet clay around them. Kissing him, entangling her tongue with his, she pushed up slightly and started to unbutton his shirt. She fumbled with one button for a time, then lifted her head, gritted her teeth, and with a frustrated grunt, ripped his shirt open to his belly, the buttons flying in all directions.

She scuttled down his body slightly and lowered her head to his chest. As the thunder continued and the stream roared only a few feet away, Longarm felt the girl's lips sucking and gently nibbling the hard, flat slabs of his chest, her hands kneading his biceps and shoulders.

Gooseflesh rose on his back and down his thighs, and his shaft throbbed against soaked denim.

"Give it to me," she groaned, raking her fingernails down his chest and across his belly, gritting her teeth.

Longarm winced at the sting, but his cock only grew harder.

The girl rolled onto her butt, clawing at her cartridge

belt. As she shucked the belt and both holsters aside, Longarm pushed to a sitting position and removed his own cartridge belt before working on the belt holding up his pants and then on his fly buttons.

As he rocked back and forth on his butt, shoving the soaked denims and underwear down his legs, the girl turned to him, breasts hanging free between the flaps of her vest, her own pants rolled down around her ankles. Her legs were long, muscled from horseback riding, and as tan as the rest of her. The wedge of fur between her thighs was the same copper as her hair. As she pushed him back to take over the job of rolling his pants down, Longarm silently remarked to himself that this little vixen had been running around buck naked in the daylight hours.

Did her father know about that?

"Oh, Jesus!" she cried on the heels of a lightning strike about a hundred yards away.

From the corner of his eye, Longarm saw sparks shower down from a rocky butte top. Thunder crashed, rattling his brain around in his skull.

The girl bent over him, icy tendrils of her soaked hair caressing his belly, and wrapped her fingers around his cock. Her head lowered farther. Longarm felt warm wet lips close over the head of his swollen shaft, felt her tongue touch the tip and trace a circular path around it until the entire organ felt like one tender, exposed nerve.

Her head rose. Her hand pumped him several agonizing times. He stretched his lips back from his teeth and pressed his hand against the muddy ground, holding himself in.

The girl straddled him brusquely, her knees pummeling his ribs. She leaned forward, kissed him as though to suck his tonsils out of his throat, then lifted her butt, reached down, and directed his shaft through the furry portal to her hot, wet core.

"Eeee-owwwww!" she screamed as Longarm hit bottom, jerking her head up, lightning again flashing in her eyes and glistening off her teeth.

She sank slowly, rose, sank again, then up more quickly . . . until, after a minute of gradually increasing her rhythm while grinding her fingers painfully into Longarm's shoulders, she was bouncing up and down on his cock with an almost frightening fury and wailing like a she-panther in profoundest heat.

They came together, both quivering as they ground their bodies together, as another lightning bolt struck a ridge on the other side of the stream. The report was like a .45 blast inside a small cave. Its echo hadn't dwindled before an enormous thunderclap racked the heavens and seemed to make even the rain hesitate before it continued plunging in slanting sheets.

The girl's head had fallen back on her shoulders, Longarm's hands squeezing her breasts. Now she dropped her chin as though her neck were broken and sagged forward, collapsing on his chest.

They lay there, half dozing. Longarm was only vaguely aware of the rain slowing.

Somewhere nearby, a heavy thump was followed by a wet sucking sound in the mud. A horse whinnied so loudly that Longarm and the girl both jerked their heads up with startled grunts. The buckskin stood only a few feet away, staring down at them, Longarm's McClellan saddle hanging beneath its belly. His bedroll and saddlebags were gone.

The horse dropped its long snout and shook its head, rattling its bridle and bit chains.

The girl straightened and, keeping one hand on his chest, used the other to pull her hair back from her face. She looked down at him, curling her upper lip wryly as she climbed to a knee, then a foot, and stepped away from him. She stooped to draw her denims up her legs.

Longarm sat up, drew up his pants, then stood and wrapped his sodden gunbelt around his waist. He reset his saddle, glad to find his rifle was still in its boot—nothing in his saddlebags couldn't be replaced—then swung up onto the buckskin's back.

The rain had slowed and the thunder was rumbling on out of the area, but distant lightning bolts continued to flash.

"You wanna look for your steeldust?" Longarm asked the girl.

Wanda Diamond shook her head and donned her muddy hat. "If he made it, he'll find his way back to the barn."

She lifted a hand to him, and Longarm swung her up onto the horse's butt. He reined the buckskin around, then gigged him north toward the big house staring down ominously from the high bluff ahead.

Chapter 8

Gunmetal clouds hovered low, spitting rain, and the thunder popped and boomed like a battle royal moving in slow, distant circles—two fierce warriors attacking and retreating only to attack and retreat again. Intermittent lightning flashed like cannon maws.

It was one of those midsummer prairie tempests that might last two or three days. Longarm hoped no cyclones dropped from those swollen, ominous clouds. He had no wish to be carried airborne to Kansas.

As he and the girl approached the bluff on which the tall, forlorn Victorian loomed, tension bit at him through his sodden fatigue and postcoital indolence.

Would he run into Loony Larry Dixon up here? And if so, how would he take him down? His guns and ammo were soaked. Even if he found a couple of dry cartridges, he couldn't haul the man back to town in this weather. Most of the coulees and washes between here and Snakehead Gap were no doubt as treacherous as the one that had nearly drowned him.

A damn fine mess.

As he and Wanda followed a switchback trail up the side

of the bluff, he decided that patience would be his best strategy here. He'd continue his impersonation of Calvin Lonnigan, aimless drifting waddie, while learning everything he could about the evildoing in these parts, then turn over his face card when his guns and cartridges had dried out and the best opportunity for not getting killed revealed itself.

The buckskin blew as it gained the ridge top. Lightning flashed and sparked, making a slashing, zinging bark to Longarm's right. The horse jumped.

As the girl suddenly tightened her grip around his waist, pressing her cheek to his back with a start, Longarm turned to see blue brimstone dancing and skipping atop a wrought-iron fence enclosing a small burial plot. Inside the fence were three arched grave stones. The largest was flanked by a small, transplanted chokecherry shrub that wasn't doing well in spite of the current downpour. Longarm squinted to read the words chiseled into the granite: Howard Clayton Diamond.

As the fiddle-footed buckskin continued toward the house, Longarm tried to keep his voice casual as he stared at the burial plot. "Your old man pass on, did he?"

The girl followed Longarm's glance, then turned to regard him wryly over his right shoulder, hair plastered to the side of her beautiful head. "We didn't bury him out here alive."

At risk of sounding suspiciously curious, Longarm asked another questions. "Who runs the ranch?"

"We do!" the girl said snootily, not bothering to explain.

The house was farther back from the lip of the butte than it had appeared from below. As they approached, Longarm saw a sprawling, three-story structure—a mansard-roofed, shake-shingled Victorian with a broad, wraparound porch and several broad, stone chimneys.

Scrollwork in various patterns adorned the place, and four fluted columns held up the porch flanked by broad windows.

It had once been spectacular, but the place was going to seed quickly. Its paint was chipped and peeling. A couple windows were webbed with cracks, two or three shutters hanging askew. One of the porch columns tilted dangerously. The white picket fence enclosing a small yard of brown weeds and dead flowers was missing several slats, and the rest needed paint as badly as the house.

As he approached one of the two wrought-iron hitch racks placed on either side of the front gate, Longarm thought the place looked brittle enough that a storm only slightly larger than the one booming around him now might scatter it like jackstraws across eastern Colorado and half of Texas.

The lawman–drifter helped the girl off the buckskin's back and glanced toward the back of the house, where he caught a glimpse of several log and adobe brick shacks and peeled log corrals scattered down the bluff's slanting crest, all looking gray and soggy in the spitting rain.

He beat rain from his hat and looked at Wanda. "I take it the bunkhouse and stables are back thataway . . ."

The girl opened the rickety gate in the fence and wheeled toward him, quirking a lusty smile and canting her head toward the house. "They are at that, but you'll be staying in the house tonight, fella. I'll send a man to tend your horse."

Longarm shrugged and glanced around the house once more. Was Loony Larry holed up in one of the outlying shacks? He looped the reins over the hitch rack and followed the girl along the crumbling cobbles, up to the porch, which was missing several floorboards, and into the house.

He hadn't yet closed the door on the grumbling storm before he heard men's voices somewhere right of the carpeted foyer. Someone shouted, "Donny, I seen you drop that Jack outta your sleeve, you son of a bitch! Now put it back in the deck or I'm gonna grease you, you cheatin' bastard!"

"Home sweet home," Wanda said, chuckling as Longarm scraped his muddy boots on the hemp rug in front of the door. "We don't fret over the house so much since Pa died."

She gave Longarm's pistol belt a coquettish tug. "Follow me."

As she led the lawman down a short hall, past a couple of open doorways and into a large parlor, he saw what she meant. The inside of the house was nearly as ragged as the outside, with peeling, exotically patterned wallpaper and a quarter-inch of dust on the obviously expensive furniture. Mud streaked the Oriental rugs. Bullet holes marred the walls and windows and a couple original oil paintings of country scenes featuring blooded horses and men and women in fancy English riding attire.

Lamps were missing mantles, tack was spread everywhere, trash was piled in corners, and the furniture was scrambled around as though to suit the whims of reveling barbarians. The massive fieldstone fireplace sitting against the right wall and under a wide, carpeted staircase was fronted with scattered feathersticks for kindling. Chunks of wood and bark and mounds of sawdust littered the carpet and oak floor in a broad area fronting the raised hearth. The fire snapped and popped and billowed smoke toward the soot-stained, wainscoted ceiling.

Above the hearth loomed a giant oil painting of an

elderly, congenial-looking gent with gray hair forming a semicircle around his domed, pink pate and curly gray muttonchops. The Diamond Bar B's affable patriarch, Howard Diamond, most likely. Someone had drilled a bullet hole through each eye.

The air was rife with the smell of wood smoke, tobacco, and charred meat and beans.

On a fainting couch angled in front of the fire, a young lady maybe eighteen or nineteen sprawled on her back, sound asleep and snoring softly. One foot dangled to the floor. With features akin to Wanda's, but with slightly darker hair and a rounder face, she wore a partly buttoned man's shirt, faded blue denims, and socks from the holes of which delicate pink toes protruded.

On the low table in front of the couch stood a half-empty bottle and a half-eaten steak sandwich. Between the bottle and the sandwich lay a Colt Navy revolver and a box spilling .44 shells.

Wanda paused to yell through a door in the room's left wall, in the direction of the men's voices and laughter. "Lyle, there's a horse needin' tendin' outside. Sanchez, I want a hot bath in my room. Plenty of water. *Comprende?*"

"*Sí, sí,* senorita!" a man yelled above the hoots and hollers of the others.

A pan rattled and a stove lid clanked.

"The queen's home!" shouted another man, voice thick with drink.

Wanda turned toward Longarm then, frowning as a thought dawned on her. She turned back to the doorway. "Bridge over Sand Creek's out! None of you boys get a wild hair and decide to take a ride in the rain!"

As the drunken conversation continued, Wanda crossed

the parlor's torn, stained carpet, angling around the haphazardly placed furniture, and glanced down at the girl on the fainting couch. "Lilly always did hate a rainy day."

She grabbed the bottle off the table and strode across the room to a stairway, the newel post of which was missing its ball. She paused to glance over the mahogany rail at Longarm, who couldn't help looking around in awe.

The house had been turned into a bunkhouse, or probably more accurately, an outlaw lair. And not a well-kept outlaw lair, at that. The old man must be spinning in his soggy grave.

"What're you waiting for, big man?" Wanda smiled smokily. "The party's upstairs."

Longarm looked at her and, in spite of himself, felt the old trouser snake rear its head once more. She was leaning forward against the rail, exposed breasts pushing up between the flaps of her vest. She chuckled and continued up the stairs and out of sight.

Longarm glanced once more at the sleeping girl, who was every bit as pretty as her sister, and at the gun on the table. He considered grabbing it—his own was probably too soaked to fire—but Wanda might find it.

Nervous as a cat in a room full of rocking chairs, hearing the heated and celebratory voices from the other side of the house—gunslicks, no doubt—Longarm clomped up the carpeted stairs in his wet boots.

He followed the stairs up past the first landing to the second, where someone had swept a pile of dirt into a corner beside a dead potted palm. The window near the plant had been broken out and boarded over, and the hall was dusky.

Behind one of the several closed doors around him, Longarm heard the grunts, sighs, and squawking bedsprings of a mattress being given a workout violent enough to bust a frame and go through a plaster wall.

He started forward, following Wanda into the hall's musty shadows. A clock ticked beneath the sounds of the lovemaking, and occasional yells could still be heard from the cardplayers below.

"Ooooo, Larrrr-yyyy!" a girl moaned behind a door somewhere ahead of Longarm.

A man grunted loudly and sucked air through his teeth as the girl loosed a shriek.

A wave of excitement rippled up and down Longarm's chilled back.

Loony Larry?

"Come on!" Wanda beckoned from a doorway on the hall's right side, directly across from the couplers.

Longarm strode into the room. Wanda threw the door closed behind him. She set the bottle on a washstand and strode toward a four-poster against the left wall, the sheets and quilts rumpled and twisted. She doffed her hat, turned to Longarm, and staring at him, her face set hard, eyes blazing with a primitive lust, she shrugged violently out of her vest.

The full breasts jostled, nipples jutting, as she tossed the vest to the floor.

Longarm stared at her. Beautiful and alluring as she was, he kept an ear pricked on the noises—chuckles and laughter and squawking floorboards—from the room across the hall.

"What's the matter?" Wanda said. "Why so shy all of a sudden?"

Longarm hiked a shoulder. "I reckon I'm just wonderin' where the hell I am. Seems a right odd ranch setup for a passel of pretty women."

"I'll play the piano for you later."

"The hired men stay in the house, do they?"

"For now, that's none of your concern. I've been hearing Aubrey and Larry going at it like a couple of minks for weeks, and I want to be fucked good and proper." She lifted her chin. "It's been a while since I had a man—a *real* man and not some sniveling man-*child*—between my legs."

She unbuttoned her denims. "Come on. Don't tell me the snake's too tired to wiggle out of its hole again." She glanced down at Longarm's bulging crotch. "I know better."

"I reckon the snake's willin'," Longarm said, his own lust pushing aside the image of Larry Dixon bounding through the door with a gun blazing in each fist. There wasn't much he could do tonight, anyway, except keep the copper-haired Wanda happy.

He walked toward her, shrugging out of his own shirt and dropping his hands to his cartridge belt. He stared down at her; she stared up at him, bare breasts rising and falling as she breathed, erect nipples edging toward his chest. "I thought your Mex was comin' with a bath. I don't like to be distracted in the middle of something important, if you know what I mean."

"You'll hardly know he's here," she said softly, still staring up at Longarm as she lifted a leg to peel her soggy denims off. "We trained him well, my sisters and I."

"A trained Mex," Longarm said, peeling off his own jeans and underwear, his soaked socks flopping around his feet. "I gotta see that to believe it."

"We hire only the best here at the Diamond spread. The best and the best-trained . . . though we like to do the training ourselves."

"Your sisters and you?"

She nodded slowly, tossed her jeans into a corner, and walked up to him, glancing appreciatively down at his jutting dong. She placed her hands on the slabs of his chest, rubbing the heels into the hard pectorals with a throaty sigh.

"Now, suppose we stop talkin', Cal." She dropped a hand to his shaft, wrapped her fingers around it, and squeezed. "Even on a rainy day, there's work to be done around here."

She dropped to her knees slowly, squeezed his shaft a few more times, and pumped it gently. Then she glanced up at him beguilingly before moving her head toward his crotch and closing her mouth over his shaft. Longarm rocked back on the balls of his feet as she licked and sucked. Pleasure rippled up and down and through his body, his head swirling, heart thudding.

She was still sucking when footsteps rose down the corridor, growing louder along with the sounds of water sloshing, a man breathing heavily.

A knock on the door. Longarm drew a startled breath.

Wanda pulled her mouth off his swollen shaft and, holding it in one hand, looked around him toward the door.

"Get in here, Sanchez!"

Longarm didn't turn as the door opened, but in the corner of his eye, he saw a short, stoop-shouldered, black-haired man amble from the door to the large, zinc-lined tub on his right and pour a bucket of steaming water into the tub. He kept his head turned away from Longarm and Wanda—with more fear than tact, Longarm judged.

"You'll need to wash our clothes, Sanchez," Wanda said. "And hurry with the rest of the water. My friend and I want some privacy."

"*Sí*, senorita," the man wheezed as he scurried out the door and off down the hall.

Wanda chuckled huskily, obviously enjoying her own power, and continued sucking Longarm like a lollipop until he thought his loins would burst.

He reached down and grabbed her shoulders. She groaned, annoyed, as he pushed her onto the bed, but then she scuttled back and spread her legs for him. She lifted her head to watch, wide-eyed, as he crawled up between her legs and directed his shaft into her core.

Longarm pummeled the girl until they were both nearly senseless and lying flat across the bed as though they'd both fallen from the sky.

The storm had snuck back around. Thunder popped and boomed like dynamite blasts, and the now-dark windows flashed with lightning.

"Jesus," the girl groaned, clutching the insides of her thighs through the sheet and quilt she pulled up over them both. "I'm gonna walk bowlegged for a week!"

Longarm wasn't sure what it was about this girl, but in spite of how tired he was, he felt another spark in his loins. Could it be that she and her beautiful sisters were running some kind of outlaw camp? Remembering the "wolf women" he'd encountered in the Front Range of the Rockies not so long ago, he reckoned it wouldn't be the first time he'd been attracted to the dark side.

He rolled over and nuzzled Wanda's breasts until her nipples pebbled once more.

She chuckled and pushed his head away. "Time for a bath."

As she began crawling toward the side of the bed, Longarm reached around from behind, grabbed her breasts in both his hands, and settled her back down on his again-hard organ grinder.

"Ohh!" she gasped.

Then, as she got comfortable and began rising up and down on her knees, her back to Longarm's head, his hands on her slender waist, she fairly howled with each dip and rise of her firm, round butt. Her damp hair hung straight down in front of her, the ends brushing across Longarm's knees.

When they came together again, fifteen minutes later, the bed slamming the wall with booms as loud as the thunder outside, she threw her head back and howled like a she-wolf on a full moon night.

Finally she exhaled wearily, turned to face him, and sagged down against his chest, running a finger across his lips then resting her hands on each side of his face, nuzzling his neck.

"As the Mexicans say," she muttered, her shoulders rising and falling as she breathed, "you are *mucho hombre*, senor."

Longarm yawned and wrapped his arms around the girl's slender back. "You ain't nothin' to trifle with yourself, amiga."

When they'd both caught their breaths, the girl lifted her head and smiled at him coquettishly. "Smoke?"

"Don't mind if I do." His three-for-a-nickel cheroots had all been ruined during his and the girl's swim.

Wanda got up and, padding barefoot around the room, her drying hair buffeting down her back and across her shoulders and jostling breasts, retrieved the bottle and two cigars. Longarm watched her, having to remind himself over and over again that he couldn't get too comfortable.

This was no New Orleans brothel, but an outlaw lair on hell's backside. He didn't have a posse armed with Gatling guns waiting out in the trees.

Wanda sagged back down on the bed, the bottle in one hand, two cigars in the other. She poked a cigar between Longarm's lips, scratched a lucifer to life on the bedpost, and lit it. When she'd lit her own cigar, she handed Longarm the bottle.

"I gotta say, Miss Wanda," Longarm said, wincing as chokecherry wine burned over his tonsils, setting a soothing fire in his chest. He gave the bottle back to the girl. "If I woulda known what life was like out here at the Diamond Bar B, I'd have come callin' a long time ago."

"Don't start thinking I'm some wanton hussy, mister." Wanda tipped back the wine then wiped her lips with the hand holding the bottle. "Papa kept a tight rein on us girls. Hardly ever let us go to town except for church. Hardly let us off the ranch except to go to school. I didn't even know what a *man's* cock looked like till a few months ago. I'm twenty-three, and I sorta feel like I got some catchin' up to do."

Longarm took the bottle back from the girl and asked with an offhand, innocently curious air, "How'd your pa die, anyway, Miss Wanda—if you don't mind my askin'?"

She slid her eyes toward him suspiciously. He tensed. He'd pushed too hard. Finally, she sighed and leaned back against the headboard, taking a deep drag off the Mexican cigar.

"Poor Pa. He started getting confused a few years back. Downright forgetful. Sometimes he'd get lost on his own range, and one of us girls would have to ride out and fetch him back. And then, when we started gettin' overrun by squatters and rustlers an' such, he chose to do nothin' about it at all.

"Pa was always generous to a fault—though he was strict with us girls—but lettin' squatters chew up our graze and steal our cattle"—Wanda chuffed caustically, and took another long pull from the wine, choking a little—"was downright loco. That's when we figured he was crazier'n a tree full of owls."

The girl gave the bottle to Longarm and inspected a cut on her mud-streaked elbow. Her pretty eyes, bleary from drink, owned a pensive air. "Then his horse fell back on him, and he had to take to bed. He was out of his head most of the time. That's when my sisters and I decided it was time to hire more riders—riders who could handle a six-shooter and a carbine. Pa didn't like that at all, said he'd have no regulators on the Diamond Bar B. Well, hell, it was either regulators or have the Bar B overrun with squatters—Norwegians, Swedes, even a Dutchman and a couple Italians.

"No, sir, we couldn't have that," Wanda said with a fateful sigh. "Finally, my sisters and I took a vote, decided it was time to put Pa out of his misery. He just wasn't himself—he wasn't enjoying life anymore—and he was doing more harm than good to the Bar B."

Longarm turned to her slowly and arched a brow. Christ, what was she going to tell him?

Wanda stared at her knees for a time, arms crossed on her breasts. He wasn't sure she was going to continue, but then she licked her lips.

"We drew straws," she said softly. "Cassie got the short one, and she went through with it, all right. I thought she was just going to smother the old man with his pillow.

91

She did that, but then she grabbed her pistol and shot him through the forehead, too."

Longarm tried not to look horrified. Her tone had been so even and matter-of-fact while delivering the horrific tale that Longarm felt a razor-edged saber tip of dread prod his spine.

"Said she wanted to make sure he wasn't suffering," Wanda continued. "I reckon he didn't suffer any more after that. We buried him up yonder—well, you saw—with Ma and his first wife, Mary Red Hand, Cassie's ma. A couple days later Larry came, and a couple days after that"—Wanda laughed, suddenly buoyant—"Aubrey married that crazy son of a bitch!"

Chapter 9

Loony Larry Dixon was here at the Diamond Bar B ranch, after all.

Longarm wasn't sure if it had thundered at the same time the girl had mentioned the killer's name, or if Longarm had just imagined it. Real or imagined, Longarm had heard thunder, and he had a feeling he was going to hear a lot more before his mission was over.

Well, he was glad he hadn't come all this way and wasted all this time in Wanda Diamond's minklike clutches for nothing. Billy Vail would never know how Longarm had spent the last couple of hours, as the deputies didn't have to account for every minute they spent on the public clock, but Longarm couldn't help feeling a tad negligent, fucking rather than cuffing, as it were.

But he had to get serious and figure out a way to throw a rope around the killer's neck and haul him back to town . . .

That wasn't happening anytime soon, however. Wanda urged him to take a bath with her—in the tub the Mexican had filled while he and the girl had been otherwise employed. They frolicked, soaping each other a little more and a little longer than necessary and getting so heated up again that they did it doggie-style on the floor beside the tub.

The girl's story about how she and her sisters had killed their father had dampened Longarm's enthusiasm considerably, but not enough so that the girl herself would have noticed.

When they'd toweled each other off, she took a long slug from the chokecherry wine—which she and her sister made themselves, she'd told him—then handed the bottle to Longarm.

"Let's go downstairs and meet the fellas you'll be working with," she said, pulling a thick, white robe out of a closet.

Longarm lowered the bottle from his lips. "Working with?"

"Sure." Wanda walked over and wrapped her hand around his red-chafed dong. "You don't think I'd let one like you get away, do you?"

Longarm held the bottle up in salute, covering a wry smile, then took another pull.

She frowned up at him. "Don't you wanna know what the pay is, or what you'll be doing?"

Longarm choked a little on the sweet, fruity wine, which tasted a little like plum mixed with rose blossoms. "I was just going to ask that."

"The pay is forty a month and found." She threw her hair back from the robe's collar, suddenly all business. "You'll be running off the squatters and shooting the rustlers. Pretty simple, as long as you follow Larry's orders. He's crazier than a shit-house rat, but he's efficient, and he's colorful if he doesn't get too drunk. He'll fill you in later."

"Sounds fine as frog hair, Miss Wanda," Longarm

said, looking around. His clothes had vanished, and then he remembered that she'd ordered the Mex to wash them. "I'm right eager to meet this Larry fella . . . but could we do it when I have my clothes back?"

Wanda rummaged around in the closet, then tossed Longarm a green plaid robe, which he held out for inspection.

"It looks a might small."

"Pa wasn't nearly as big as you, but it should cover all the important parts." She laughed again and grabbed the wine bottle off the dresser. "I don't want Aubrey to get a look at that donkey dong of yours, or she'll be wanting me to share!"

Longarm reached for his gun belt out of habit.

"You won't be needin' that," Wanda said, setting the bottle down and heading for the door. "You're among friends here, cowboy."

Longarm didn't feel nearly as foolish in the green plaid robe that didn't quite cover his wrists or shins when, descending the stairs barefoot behind the copper-haired Wanda, he saw five men and three young women lounging about the parlor in as compromising attire as his own.

The girls were all in wrappers or pantaloons, and the one who'd been passed out earlier on the fainting couch had night ribbons in her thick brown hair. She was curled up on another couch, her head in the lap of a wiry, blond rannie who couldn't have been much over seventeen.

He was clad in only a white undershirt and longhandles, a red and white neckerchief knotted around his sunburned neck. He had a shabby bowler on his head and a cornhusk cigarette burning between his lips.

Two glistening, silver-plated Remington revolvers lay

beside him on the couch, with the oily rag he'd apparently cleaned them with. At his feet was a freshly soaped saddle.

The blond-headed rannie and the girl, Lilly, who'd been reading a dime novel, looked up as Wanda and Longarm descended the stairs. The other two girls were lounging around with two of the other four men, while the two loners played poker on the far side of the room.

A fire roared in the hearth, sending smoke and occasional sparks into the room. Judging by the poor draw, the chimney hadn't been cleaned in many months. The smoky room was lit by the fire and several lamps and candles. Lightning continued to flash in the windows, the panes of which were streaked with rain.

With one hand on the newel post, Wanda announced, "Boys, girls, meet Cal Lonnigan, a new friend of mine. Put your drinks and cards down and try to look like you weren't all raised in creek bottoms and sow pens."

"Ain't nothin' wrong with a sow pen, Miss Wanda," said one of the two men playing cards on a small, decorative table that had no doubt cost a pretty penny at one time but that now, scraped and scarred and marred with cigarette burns, was good for little more than kindling. "It's a hell of a lot better than Nebraska!" The man— short and chubby-faced and wearing only duck trousers and a vest—smirked at the blond-headed lad now sizing up Longarm with slitted eyes and curled lips. "It's better than Nebraska."

The kid's sunburned face turned red and his nostrils flared, but he held his pellet-sized, belligerent green eyes on Longarm. Longarm didn't think it was anything personal. Like a dog or a bull elk, the kid probably had a bone to pick with everyone he met.

"Shut up, Moose," said the other cardplayer, head turned to regard Longarm and the girl. "I wanna meet the hombre causin' such a ruckus up yonder." He spread a snaggle-toothed grin under his walrus mustache and tipped his felt sombrero back off his pockmarked forehead. "Ain't heard Miss Wanda hoot and howl like that in a month of Sundays!"

If Wanda was embarrassed by the remark, she gave no indication. She introduced her sisters—Lilly, sitting on the couch with the blond, bowler-hatted rannie; Aubrey, sitting at the couch's other end, leaning on its arm and holding a speckled tin cup in her hand; and Cassie, sitting on the lap of a tall, bearded gent near the fire, her arms around the man's neck, a sleepy look in her eyes. She was darker than the other girls, and round-faced, with long, Indian-black hair.

Her eyes slanted devilishly as she ran her gaze up and down Longarm's large frame, which was threatening to bust out of the late Howard Diamond's robe. "To keep my sister occupied so long up yonder, you sure must know your business, mister. Wanda, she usually gets bored mighty fast!"

She grinned, brown eyes almost crossing. The man whose lap she sat on dropped his lids slowly over his drink-bleary eyes and moved his shoulders, silently chuckling. A rifle leaned against the green chair he shared with the girl, whose pretty, brown legs straddled one of his own.

Even though Cassie's eyes were as impudent as her sisters', Longarm had a hard time imagining such a lovely, dusky-skinned, dimple-cheeked sprite smothering her father with a pillow and drilling a slug through his head for good measure.

"Forgive Cassie her farm manners," Wanda said to

Longarm. "It's the Indian in her, her ma being Kiowa. The rest of us girls come from a high-bred Irish gal, though none of us knew her on account of her dyin' while delivering Aubrey."

Wanda's tone had grown vaguely accusatory as she glanced at the honey-eyed beauty sitting alone at the far end of the couch from Lilly and the blond rannie in the bowler hat. The kid's angry eyes were still sizing up Longarm as though the lawman were a horse he was deciding whether or not he should try riding.

Aubrey smiled sheepishly and hiked a shoulder. "Welcome, Cal. Daddy's robe don't fit you too good." She giggled.

It was Longarm's turn to shrug and smile sheepishly, feigning a casual air. "It's a little cool for the winter but just right for the summer."

While the girls were lovely, it was the men he scrutinized. All four looked like average owlhoots and gunslicks, and Longarm thought he'd seen a couple of the faces on Wanted dodgers here or there. Judging by their seedy looks alone, he wouldn't have trusted any of them as far as he could have thrown them uphill in a stiff wind—but none met the description of Loony Larry Dixon.

Wanda introduced the blond rannie as L.J. He continued staring owlishly at Longarm as she rattled off the names of the other three—Moose and Harlan, playing cards, and Lyle, sitting with Cassie. Only Moose said hi, while Harlan gave only a slow nod of his head, his suety, pink face implacable as he held his cards with one hand and rubbed his patch beard speculatively with the other. Lyle appeared to be asleep with his eyes open, staring into the fire with the half-breed girl on his lap.

The girls continued staring up at Longarm, the new

98

bull in the stable, as though they were considering whether or not they should contest their sister for him.

"Where's Larry?" Wanda asked, taking the words right out of Longarm's head.

"His turn to fetch wood," said the man called Moose, who slapped down a card with a chuckle.

As his opponent, Harlan, sent a scalding curse across the table to Moose, Wanda glanced at Longarm. "Make yourself comfortable, get to know the boys. I'll tell Sanchez to fry us a couple of steaks."

When she'd disappeared, Longarm stood there at the bottom of the stairs, not far from the popping fire, rolling his eyes around. Clad as he was, and unarmed, he felt like the only bird at a turkey shoot. He tried to think of something to say, but the only ones looking at him were the girls and the bowler-hatted L.J., who sat with Lilly's head on his lap, sucking the quirley between his lips and taking occasional pulls from the tequila bottle resting on the sofa arm to his left. On the couch's other end, the golden-haired Aubrey sat staring at Longarm, a wistful smile on her lips as she wound a lock of hair around her finger.

She had a mole on her chin, another just above and left of the bridge of her nose, and they somehow added to her look of wide-eyed innocence—though the low-cut top billowing out to expose nearly all of one full, matronly breast belied the look.

Longarm picked out a chair and was making for it, feeling self-conscious in the robe and his bare feet, when the fire reared up with a sudden draft. A distant door slammed, as though someone had come in from outside. As Longarm made his way to a leather chair on the room's right end—his ears pricked, his eyes keen, and the nerves dancing along the surface of his skin—he heard the rising scuff of soft-soled shoes. Someone was dragging his heels as he approached the parlor.

As the scuffs grew louder, Longarm stopped, one arm on the back of the chair he'd been heading toward, to turn with feigned casualness toward the other end of the parlor. A man appeared out of the hall shadows, scuffing through the door and angling toward the fireplace, an armload of split wood in front of his chest.

Longarm blinked as though to clear his vision, his gaze glued on the medium-tall gent with long, blue white hair falling from beneath the brim of his bullet-crowned, floppy-brimmed, felt hat. Loony Larry Dixon was so absurdly dressed that he made Longarm look as though he were ready to mount up and pound leather.

The man wore a black silk kimono emblazoned with purple stars and bright yellow moons. Over each breast was stitched the outline of a howling wolf. The kimono fell to just above the man's knees, revealing his pale, slightly bowed legs covered with hair the same white as that on his head and curling onto his shoulders.

On his feet was a pair of deerskin slippers lined with rabbit fur.

Around his waist, holding the kimono tight against his flat belly, was a cartridge belt and two cross-draw holsters filled with matched, bone-gripped .44s. There was a knife sheath attached to the right holster's far side, and a stout knife handle jutted above the pistol's grips.

Longarm slumped into his chair as the kimono-clad hombre, who could be none other than Loony Larry Dixon himself, dropped the logs on the floor in front of the fire. "That's the last of the dry wood in the shed, since you idjits didn't repair the roof like you was supposed . . ." As he straightened, brushing his hands together, his ice blue eyes

100

found Longarm sitting in the overstuffed leather chair, and the skin above the bridge of his nose wrinkled abruptly.

"Who's this?" he grunted. The eyes beneath the broad hat brim, which was troughed slightly in the middle, burrowed into Longarm like hot brands through calf hide.

"Don't get your back up, Larry." Wanda stood in the doorway through which she'd disappeared a minute ago, folding her arms on her breasts as she leaned against the doorjamb, and cocked a hip. "Just a stray dog who saved my life twice this afternoon, that's all." She glanced at Longarm. "Cal Lonnigan, meet Larry Dixon. Larry's the ramrod of this outfit."

"And my man," Aubrey said, smiling love-struck across the room at Larry.

Longarm dipped his chin to his chest in cordial greeting, curling his toes under his bare feet self-consciously.

"Stray dog, eh?" Larry said, his glassy eyes still burning, his thin, pink lips forming a straight line beneath the snow-white mustache drooping down both corners of his mouth, the ends falling a good two inches below his jaw.

In a blur of motion, he snaked his right hand across his belly, grabbed the .44 from the holster on his left hip, and brought it high and forward, clicking the hammer back and aiming straight across the room at Longarm. He squinted one eye as he sighted down the barrel and gritted his teeth with fury.

"Stray *law*dog, more like!"

Chapter 10

The tail end of Larry Dixon's last sentence hadn't ceased booming and echoing around the room before the four other hard cases had bolted out of their seats, grabbed the nearest rifle or revolver, and dropping to a knee or crouching and spreading their feet, brought their weapons to bear on Longarm.

Sucking a slow breath and steeling himself for certain death, the lawman sat in his chair like a big, leathery featured statue with still-damp brown hair and clad in an undersized green plaid robe from which his hands and feet stuck out, appearing two sizes larger than they actually were. He wished he'd at least pocketed his gold-plated derringer instead of leaving it upstairs in his soggy boot.

"I knew it!" the blond rannie, L.J., hissed. "I just knew there was somethin' rotten about that son of a bitch!"

"Hold steady on him, boys." Larry moved slowly toward Longarm as he stared down his Remington's seven-and-a-half-inch barrel, the hem of the black kimono buffeting about his pale legs. "He so much as twitches a finger, burn him down!"

Longarm stayed in the chair, his expression hard, but

103

inwardly he intoned, "Shit!" over and over again and imagined his revolver lying on the dresser upstairs where he'd left it, and the rifle he'd left in his saddle boot because it was farm manners not to bring a long gun into someone's house. He was beginning to think he could have handled this situation much better than he had, and next time—if there would be a next time—he was going to keep his pecker in his pants when hunting crazy killers on land owned by beautiful women.

And he'd keep his gun buckled around his waist.

The only weapon he had was his acting skills. Slowly raising his hands and furrowing his brows, he glanced around the men as though they were all as crazy as Loony Larry. "Listen, pard, I been called many things, but a lawman ain't one of 'em."

Loony Larry drew within ten feet of the lawman's chair, and stopped. The other men stood near where they'd been sitting, aiming their weapons at Longarm's head.

Wanda stood in front of the doorway, arms hanging straight down at her sides, a shocked, incredulous look on her suntanned face. Her sisters remained where they'd been when Larry had hauled down on Longarm, regarding him as though they were watching a slow train wreck, vaguely confused and wondering what would happen next, who would be killed or mangled.

Larry laughed raucously. It was a high-pitched, faintly girlish laugh. "Who you tryin' to fool, you lyin' sack of burning dog shit? I seen you in Abilene back in '72, and you were wearin' a badge. A *federal* badge! Now I don't know whose court you were ridin' for then or whose you're ridin' for now, but I'll guaran-damn-tee you one thing, mister, you're ridin' days are over!"

He turned his head to regard Wanda frowning at the

other end of the room. "You're gonna wanna clean yourself up good, boss lady. Yessir, you done spread your legs for a lawman!" He laughed again as he turned to stare down his Remington's barrel. With a flourish, he lifted his left hand to pinch his nose with his thumb and index finger. "Better boil ya up some lye and vinegar—that's the only way to get rid of skunk spray and the bear-piss stench of federal law!"

Longarm didn't know if the man had really seen him in Abilene in '72 or not, but if he had, he had a hell of a lot better memory than Longarm had, and Longarm had been memorizing names and faces on Wanted dodgers for a long time.

Longarm kept his tone even, eyes hard as gun steel. "You're mistaken, partner. I've never *been* to Abilene, *with* a badge or *without*. I hear it's nice, though, so maybe I'll visit sometime. But back in '72 *and* '73, I was in Dakota, wranglin' for Hans Brickman."

Hans Brickman was an actual rancher in western Dakota Territory. Though Longarm had never worked for the man, he'd gotten to know him when he was up in Dakota running down stock thieves a few years back.

"Ole Hans, eh?" Larry cocked his face to one side and slitted an eye. "He still have that ramrod—what's his name? Streeter?"

Longarm shook his head though he was far from certain. He was gambling that Loony Larry was blowing smoke. "A little German, even shorter than Hans, named Schwartz. Leo Schwartz. Threw back many a vodka shot with Leo in the Pyramid Park Saloon."

Longarm stared up at Larry, who continued staring down at him. In the periphery of the lawman's vision, he could see Wanda still standing in front of the doorway, her face slightly flushed, brows furrowed. He sensed that if Larry concluded that she had indeed been deceived, she'd take Loony Larry's revolver and drill a couple of rounds into Longarm's forehead herself . . . and spit on his carcass.

A slow smile grew on the madman's face, stretching his lips and crinkling his eyes. "Ah, hell." He lifted the Remington's barrel and depressed the hammer. His tone was falsely self-deprecating. "I reckon I was wrong. I do apologize. Reckon the ole memory ain't what it used to be. The man I seen in Abilene, come to think of it, was a redheaded fella . . . and not near as tall as you appear to be."

As the other men, sliding their edgy, incredulous gazes between Longarm and Loony Larry, began lowering their own weapons, Longarm offered an affable smile, and shrugged. "Happens to all of us."

"Jesus Christ, Larry!" Wanda said. "You 'bout gave me a stroke. If I'd spent half the afternoon upstairs fucking a lawdog, I'd have gone out to the barn and hanged myself!"

With that, she swung around and disappeared into the shadows of the hallway from which the smell of frying steak and potatoes emanated as well as the sound of a man singing softly in Spanish while pans clattered and a pump squawked.

The rain continued ticking against the windows.

"Lar-ryyy!" Aubrey said, lightly admonishing, chuckling with fond amusement.

The other hard cases sighed and cursed and, guns clicking as they depressed the hammers, returned to their previous diversions—all but the kid, who muttered something about using the privy as he stomped across the room in his stocking feet.

Larry chuckled and twirled the big Remington. "Can't be too careful." He let the oiled weapon drop smoothly into its holster. "There'll be federals prowling around after them two perverts I had to give the chicken treatment. I thought maybe you was one. But then, they'd be crazy to send just *one*."

Longarm's heart was still beating crazily, and chilly sweat trickled down his spine. He turned to the crazy killer striding back over to the popping fire in his ridiculous kimono.

"Perverts?"

"A couple badge toters were out here, sneakin' a peek in the window of a line shack while Aubrey and I were doin' the big nasty!" Larry grabbed a couple of split logs from the pile he'd brought in and shoved them onto the grate.

He turned to Longarm sharply, genuine astonishment in his watery blue eyes. "Can you imagine that? Can you imagine a couple of public servants ogling private citizens—*married* private citizens—engaged in carnal frolic?"

The gunnie named Moose chuckled and shook his head as he picked up the cards Harlan was dealing. "Oh, boy . . . here we go . . ."

Larry narrowed his gaze at Longarm. "Imagine how you'd feel if someone had been upstairs, watching you slam the plank to Miss Wanda earlier. Say the Mex had left the door open a crack, and someone was *watchin'*."

Longarm winced and rubbed his jaw as he stared back at the killer's insane gaze. "I'd feel right violated . . . I reckon."

"Those lawdogs from town was out here to arrest you, Larry," Harlan said reasonably.

"Maybe they was, but they coulda waited till we was done fuckin'."

Larry shoved a couple more logs onto the fire, then stood, brushing his hands on the kimono and staring into the fire. "Yessir, I gave 'em the chicken treatment and sent 'em back to town." His shoulders moved as he laughed silently. "As a message to those that would follow."

He swung around toward Longarm, pale features flushed with fury, close-set eyes wrinkled. "Anyone fucks with me or fucks with anyone associated with this ranch loses their hat! I done employed the tactic out in Oregon a few years back, and I must say, it was right *effective*!"

Aubrey and the other two girls giggled. Lilly clutched her head and, giggling, said, "*Ow!* That's gotta *hurt*!"

"It does if they're still kickin' when you employ the tactic," Larry told her seriously. "But most times they're already dead. It's just a message to others that would follow."

Longarm couldn't shed the feeling that Loony Larry was still addressing him—one who had followed. He felt a crick in his neck.

He had to get his hands on a dry gun soon or at least on some dry loads for his own revolver. A few of his own cartridges were probably sealed tight enough that they'd fire, but he couldn't chance it. Before morning, he needed dry ammo. It wouldn't hurt to give his Colt a thorough cleaning, either, to rid the barrel and cylinders of mud and grime it had no doubt picked up in the flooded gully.

He looked at Loony Larry, who'd finished feeding the fire and was reclining beside Aubrey, nuzzling the girl's neck and sticking his hand down her shirt. "I found the rabbit," he chuckled, his voice grating, almost girlish.

"It's not *your* rabbit, Larry!" the girl said in the voice

of a three-year-old. She shoved Larry's hat off and ran her hands over the top of his head, which, between the tufts of wavy white hair, was as hairless as a baby's ass. "It's *my* rabbit!"

"And there's another," the madman shrilled as Longarm eyed the bone-gripped Remington jutting from the holster on the man's left hip. "I got two big, ole, one-eyed rabbits for the price of one!"

Mercifully, Longarm's unarmed evening with the owl-hoots passed quickly.

Soon after Larry had started nuzzling Aubrey on the love seat, Wanda returned from the kitchen with two big chipped china plates covered with thick steaks and fried potatoes. She sat crosswise on Longarm's lap, resting her head against his shoulder as they ate.

Longarm was surprised to find that he was still hungry in spite of the nerves that had started jumping around in his belly as soon as he'd crossed the big Victorian's threshold. But he managed to finish off the plate and swab up the last of the greasy potatoes with a chunk of bread, and he probably would have dug into a piece of apple cobbler and whipped cream, had one been offered.

Later, after the others had drifted off to bed by ones and twos, Wanda and Longarm took a couple of pulls from a whiskey bottle. Then drowsy from food and liquor, the girl led Longarm back upstairs. She was so tired that, to Longarm's relief, she didn't demand to be serviced again. Wrapping her hand proprietarily around his limp cock, she slumped down against his shoulder and almost immediately began snoring.

When she'd been snoring for a good twenty minutes, and the muffled snores of the others rose up and down the hallway outside her room, Longarm managed to gently slip out from under her head and hand and pad quietly over to the green plaid robe he'd hung on the door hook. He reached into the pocket and pulled out the box of .44 shells he'd slipped off a cluttered chair as Wanda had led him to bed.

His heart quickened. He moved to the dresser where he'd left his gun, his heart beating even faster as he stared down at the dresser's scarred surface.

The gun and holster were gone.

Chapter 11

Longarm slept like a man hearing his own gallows being built.

When the dawn light touched the room's single, curtained window, and a meadowlark chirped happily in the soggy yard below, he threw the covers back and dropped his feet to the floor. He sucked a deep breath and stretched his arms high above his head.

Somehow, today, he'd separate Loony Larry Dixon from his fellow cold-steel artists and from the girls, and haul him back to Snakehead Gap. No doubt the other men were wanted as well, and the girls, having hired Larry, were as guilty as Larry, but Longarm had to eat the apple one bite at a time.

And collaring Loony Larry would be one hell of a large bite.

He glanced at the dresser where his gunbelt and .44 were no longer lying. Collaring Larry would be an even bigger task without his gun. At least his clothes—all washed, dried, and ironed, and minus only his hat, which he'd lost in the flood—lay in a neat pile atop the dresser, his boots arranged below, cleaned and polished.

The poor Mex who worked for these girls was tireless.

Longarm began to rise but stopped when Wanda groaned and rolled toward him, snaked an arm around his waist, and splayed her fingers across his belly. She lowered the hand slowly to his crotch and wrapped her fingers around his cock.

First things first.

Longarm turned over and rolled on top of her. He was no longer in the mood for the girl, but he was pretty good at faking it. He swept her sleep-mussed hair back from her eyes and kissed her silky, sleep-swollen lips.

"I seem to be missing my gun," he said, and kissed her again as though only as concerned as any other man in this country would be about a missing sidearm.

When he drew his lips from hers, she lifted her head slightly to glance at the dresser. "Larry probably took it. He'll give it back when he's sure about you. I'm so glad he's here to tend to the details. Really frees me up for other things . . . if you get my drift."

She lay her head back against the pillow once more and wrapped her arms around his neck. Smiling lustily, she arched her back, wiggled her crotch against his, and wrapped her legs around his waist, squeezing. "Besides, the only gun you're gonna need for the next half hour is that one right there!"

Breakfast was no more formal an affair than anything else around the dilapidated Victorian. Eight wranglers wandered up from the bunkhouse, and some of them and a couple of Loony Larry's men—several of whom Longarm had not yet been introduced to—sat around the large dining room table, which had no doubt seen its share of formal settings but which now was as scarred as the bar of a backwater saloon.

Most of the men, however, scarfed their food on the porch to get a good look at the day, as did Wanda and Aubrey. The girls were dressed much like the men, in rough range clothes, dusters, broad-brimmed hats, and with braces of .45s decorating their curvy hips.

The storm had moved on, and, as the sun touched the eastern horizon with a brick red glow, a few last stars twinkled faintly in a sky clean and clear as a freshly laid egg.

After a brief discussion between Loony Larry and Wanda as to the day's assignments, Larry threw back the last of his coffee, dropped his cigarette stub in the cup, and glanced at Longarm.

"Lonnigan, you, me, L.J., and Harlan are gonna ride south along the creek. Wanda's gonna lead the rest of you boys and the girls west, over to where them damn Germans are settin' up camp on our fourth water hole."

Larry chuckled and shuttled his washed-out, bloodshot eyes between Longarm and Wanda. "You two think you can be apart for a few hours without bleating like lost little lambs?"

"We'll make do," Wanda said, glancing at Longarm. "You boys go ahead and spend the day together, get acquainted. You and me, we got tonight, Cal."

"Can't wait, darlin'," Longarm said, feigning a grin. His dong was so chafed that the thought of coupling with any woman again—even Cynthia Larimer—made his jaws ache with dread. With one hip hiked atop the porch rail, he picked a sliver of sausage out from between his teeth and turned to the Bar B's crazy ramrod. "What kinda business down south?"

"You'll see."

"How 'bout my gun?"

"What about it?" Loony Larry grinned.

Holding Longarm's gaze, he lifted his bullet-crowned hat to run a hand over the pink, egglike crown of his bald head, then threw back his hair and moseyed down the veranda steps and out to the front fence gate. Two half-breed boys, one maybe fourteen, the other a few years older, were leading eight or nine saddled horses, including Longarm's buckskin, around from the house's north side, along a well-worn path through the Spanish bayonet and buckbrush.

"After you, Lonnigan."

Longarm turned. The man named Harlan stood to his right, grinning through his thin red beard and holding his open hand out over the porch steps. Maintaining the grin, he said in a low, hard voice, "Me, I don't give my back to a man till I've gotten to know him real good . . . even if he ain't heeled!"

"That goes for me, too," said the kid, L.J., standing beside Harlan. He wore his bowler hat and a brown wool vest over a crisp white shirt and wide red tie. On his lean hips were his brace of silver-plated Remingtons tied low on his thighs.

Longarm shrugged and tried to leech the sarcasm from his voice as he said, "I'll be lookin' forward to the day when I can rightly say I've won you boys' trust and friendship."

He moved on down the steps and along the cobblestone walk still puddled from the heavy rain. As he approached the buckskin, which the half-breeds had tied to one of the hitch racks, he saw that his saddle boot was empty. Not surprising, but frustrating just the same.

114

His only weapon was the double-barreled derringer snugged in the small sheath sewn into the top of his right boot. He doubted that, until it was cleaned and freshly loaded, it would even fire.

A damn fine pickle you got yourself into now, Long, he silently chided himself as he climbed into the leather.

"Good-bye, Larry!" Aubrey called from the front porch, waving, as Larry spurred his claybank out toward the small cemetery at the lip of the bluff. "See you tonight, hon!"

"Later, sugar!" Larry called, waving his hat.

Standing beside her, Wanda turned to Longarm, pinched the brim of her man's felt hat, threw her shoulders back, and stuck her breasts out. Longarm waved and grinned and gigged his horse after Loony Larry, Harlan, and L.J., trailing a few feet behind.

"Shit," L.J. said. "My Lilly's prob'ly crawled back in bed."

"No doubt." Harlan laughed above the thuds of their horses' hooves on the soggy, muddy trail. "She's probably right now snugglin' up with one of the waddies from the bunkhouse!"

L.J. told Harlan to do something physically impossible to himself, then hipped around to cast a worried look back toward the house dwindling behind them.

With Loony Larry riding point and Longarm behind him followed by the other two, the foursome rode down the butte along the switchback trail that was washed out in several places and littered with eroded rock.

As the sun climbed and the air warmed and turned uncomfortably humid after the rain, the party cut cross-country, angling southeast over the rolling prairie cut here and there with draws and ravines in which floodwater still

115

flowed, though not nearly as swiftly as that which had grabbed Longarm and Wanda.

Crossing one such ravine, through water that now rose only to the buckskin's knees, Longarm saw a drowned cow hung up on a sandbar, its red brown fur glistening wet in the sunshine. Larry and the other two men paid little attention. They weren't stockmen but hired guns. The Bar B's cattle were the concern of the girls and their waddies, most of whom were relegated to the bunkhouse.

Larry and his crew were apparently here only to kill and fuck.

As the party crossed a narrow valley between camelbacks, their horses splashing through a slough around which red-winged blackbirds chirped raucously, Longarm glanced at Dixon's saddle boot. It contained two rifles—a Sharps carbine and Longarm's Winchester '73.

The lawman cursed under his breath. Was his Colt .44 in the crazy bastard's saddlebags? Sometime today, one way or another, he was going to find out.

Someone cleared his throat, and Longarm glanced over his right shoulder. The red-bearded man he knew only as Harlan trotted his pinto off the buckskin's right hip. Grinning with bright-eyed mockery, the man slid his left hand back to touch the walnut grips of the Schofield revolver riding in a fawn-colored holster decorated with turquoise Indian beads. He gave the gun a pat, glanced at Longarm's naked hip, then winked and threw his head back, laughing.

Longarm smiled woodenly and shook his head. "A real joker," he muttered beneath the splashing hooves. "When I get my hands on my own irons, I'm gonna drill one up your ass, show ya how much I've enjoyed your company."

116

After an hour of steady riding, Dixon drew to a halt at the lip of a low ridge and raised his hand for the others to follow suit. Longarm glanced once more at his Winchester snugged in the man's saddle boot, then drew his own horse up to the lip of the ridge.

Shielding his eyes from the brassy sun, he peered into the brushy hollow on the other side, bordered in the background by high, bald, dome-topped buttes. Directly below, a small cabin of vertical, whipsawed pine boards stood behind a brush-roofed veranda. Surrounded by twenty or thirty grazing cattle, it was flanked by a privy and two corrals of unpeeled cottonwood logs. A couple of mules and a paint horse milled inside the corral.

Smoke curled from the cabin's tin chimney pipe. A shaggy brown and white dog lay on the porch, head between its paws, asleep.

In the yard before the cabin, two men in washworn denims were digging with shovels. A third lay in the flatbed of a spring wagon. The man was covered with several empty feed sacks, but parts of two lace-up boots protruded from beneath the sacks, to stick a good half foot out over the end of the wagon bed.

Dixon shook his head with disgust, jostling his long, white hair across his shoulders. "Sons o' bitches are still here." He glanced at L.J. and Harlan, his pale face flushed with fury. "Now I done honored Wanda's wishes to ease those bastards on out of here. Gave 'em ample warnin', since they were friends of ole Mr. Diamond himself." He rose up in his stirrups and threw out an arm, pointing toward the cabin as he shuttled his gaze between L.J. and Harlan. "But what am I sitting here and staring at today?"

He continued staring at the other two men, as if awaiting

an answer. L.J. wriggled around in his saddle uncomfortably, glanced at Harlan, then said without confidence, "Them. They're . . . still here . . ."

"That's right they're still here, goddamnit!" Dixon dropped his hand to his thigh and spat with frustration. "They did not heed my warning nor honor the girls' wishes for them to haul ass off Bar B range. So now I got one hell of a dirty job to do!"

In the middle of the crazy man's tirade, the shaggy dog had lifted its head and, turning toward the ridge overlooking the small ranch yard, gained its feet and started barking angrily, tail cocked high. The men digging the grave had stopped digging to turn toward the ridge, as well.

Now, as Dixon and the others scowled into the hollow, the taller of the two grave diggers kicked his shovel into the fresh mound of wet dirt and, keeping an eye on the ridge, sauntered over to the wagon. He reached up under the seat and pulled out a long-barreled shotgun. Keeping his eyes on the ridge, he leaned the shotgun against the wagon's left front wheel, then moseyed back over to where the other man stood, holding his shovel and staring up at the ridge.

The man holding the shovel—lean-bodied, long-faced, and wearing a red and black checked shirt under a brown cowhide vest—wore a revolver in a holster hanging low on his right hip. He wasn't wearing a hat, and his thin, gray black hair slid around in the breeze.

"I believe those boys are armed," Longarm said, rubbing his jaw and sliding his gaze toward Loony Larry. "And they don't look happy to see us. Now might be a good time to turn over a hogleg, Dixon."

"Couldn't hurt," Harlan grunted at Loony Larry, shrugging. "Ain't much point for him to ride with us if we don't give him a gun."

Larry turned sharply to both Longarm and Harlan and said with strained patience, nostrils flaring, "When I get a good *feel* about him, I'll give him a gun. Till then, I want you both to shut the fuck up!"

He reined his claybank left with an exasperated shake of his head and gigged it down the ridge. *"Christ!"*

Chapter 12

Longarm held back on the buckskin's reins until the other two riders, more preoccupied now with the men in the hollow than with their new partner, had gigged their own mounts down the ridge behind Dixon.

Then he turned the buckskin down the horse trail as well, the mount's hooves slipping and sliding in the wet clay. As he and the others bottomed out in the swale and started across the muddy stream sliding along the base of the ridge, the dog had come out from the house to bark and growl on the stream's other side. As Dixon, Harlan, L.J., and Longarm heeled their mounts into the water, the dog lowered its head and drew its ears back, barking viciously, curling its tail up over its back and bouncing forward on its front paws.

The two grave diggers stood before the mound of freshly dug mud. The one wearing the holstered revolver leaned on his shovel while the other, a taller, black-bearded man, stood within reach of the shotgun leaning against the wagon's left front wheel. A stout woman in a sack dress stood frozen in the cabin's doorway, a towel in one hand, a pan in the other.

"Get away, pooch!" Dixon snarled as the dog stood on the bank just ahead and to his right, barking even more viciously than before.

"Blaze!" the black-bearded gent called, lifting his chin. "Come on, boy!"

"Call your goddamn dog off!" Harlan yelled, scowling down at the dog as his horse gained the muddy shore. "He comes at me, I'm gonna shoot the son of a bitch!"

"Blaze!" the black-bearded man shouted. "Get over here!"

"Goddamnit," Dixon grunted, reaching around his belly to grab his Colt from the cross-draw holster on his left hip.

As his horse lunged up the stream bank beside Harlan, Dixon cocked his revolver and extended it out over his claybank's right hip. The dog bolted forward at the same time that Dixon's revolver popped. The slug plunked into the mud six inches behind the dog, and the dog yelped loudly, wheeled, and galloped back toward the house—a brown and white streak in the knee-high wheatgrass.

Dixon cursed again. "Can't stand dogs." He reined the claybank to a halt, cocked and extended his Colt once more, and tracked the fleeing animal.

K-pop!

The bullet spanged off a rock just behind the dog, spurring the animal into an even faster sprint for the cabin. As the dog ducked under the porch, the woman standing in the doorway half closed the door in front of her, as if to shield herself from another bullet.

Chuckling, Dixon holstered his Colt and gigged the claybank forward, Harlan urging his own horse about ten yards right of Dixon's. The owl-eyed youngster, L.J., drew his Winchester carbine from his saddle scabbard and pulled his roan up to Dixon's left. The three men, swaying easily and smugly in their saddles, walked their horses toward the men standing grimly by the grave.

Dixon glanced over his shoulder at Longarm bringing up the rear. "Come on, Lonnigan. Gonna introduce you to some friends of mine."

Longarm kneed the buckskin toward the two grave diggers. His belly burned. Dixon was going to kill these men and probably the woman, and without a gun, there wasn't a damn thing the lawman could do about it.

As the buckskin moved forward and the other three men spread out ahead of him, Longarm eyed his rifle snugged down in Dixon's saddle boot. His derringer wasn't much, but it was something. Keeping his eyes forward, he slowly reached down and plucked the peashooter from the sheath in his right boot well. He palmed the gold-plated pistol, then slipped it behind the waistband of his denims.

As he drew his horse up between Dixon on his right and Harlan on his left, the two grave diggers eyed him and the others with pursed lips and slitted eyes. L.J. swung his horse toward the wagon on the other side of the grave and right, and stopped the horse near the boots of a dead man sticking out over the end of the box. Smiling as though he were heading to a rodeo to spark the neighbor girls, the kid held his carbine negligently across his saddle bows.

Loony Larry Dixon poked his hat brim off his forehead and regarded the two men before him in grim silence.

"Well, well, Mr. Patten," he said finally. "It is a sad surprise to see you here. A sad, sad surprise."

"Don't know why it'd be such a surprise," the older man snapped, his jaw set hard as he leaned on his shovel. "I done told you last week I wasn't pullin' foot. I don't

123

care how fast you are, or how many guns you got ridin' with ya. I filed on this land legal, goddamnit! Mr. Diamond had no quarrel with me bein' here. I don't why you"—his jaws tightened and his eyes pinched—"or them *girls* of his should."

"The girls are expandin' their herd, Mr. Patten," Dixon said. "Done told you that. They got bigger dreams than the old man did. Movin' more cattle in from all over. We're gonna need this graze here, and that water, 'fore long."

The black-bearded gent closed one eye and turned his head slightly to stare suspiciously up at Loony Larry. "And where you suppose they're gettin' them extra beef?"

"I don't s'pose nothin'," Dixon said, grinning slightly as he lifted his gaze to the white-faced cattle gnawing the wheat grass around the ranch headquarters and along the slopes on the other side of the creek. The smile faded quickly as he returned his gaze to the black-bearded man. "I *know* where they come from. And I know where they're goin', too—to the Indian agency over in Kansas." His insolent smile broadened. "Injuns gotta eat, too. And, whooee, you know how much the government pays for beef?"

Patten opened his mouth to speak, but the kid, L.J., suddenly reached over the wagon box and pulled one of the feed sacks away from the body, revealing the dead man's pale face capped with black, carefully combed hair. The man's white shirt was buttoned to his throat, and the ends of his black mustache were waxed to points.

The black-bearded man shouted, "Get away from there!"

L.J. laughed as, swinging his carbine's barrel toward the black-bearded gent, he stared down at the body in the wagon box. "Hey, where'd the stiff come from?"

"Our hired man," Patten growled. "His horse threw

him in the creek last night. Couldn't swim a lick, the poor bastard."

"That's a damn shame," Loony Larry said, turning his mouth corners down with mock sadness.

"Oh, yeah?" Patten said. "Why you so sad?"

"It makes me sad," Dixon said, abruptly hardening his voice again, "because I wanted to kill that son of a bitch myself. Wanted to drill a hole through his brisket, then cut his head off. It shore woulda looked pretty . . . all three of your heads and the woman's head and that fuckin' *cur's* head all lined up together on your porch rail for the neighbors to find!"

He slapped his thigh as he laughed with glee. "But that's no nevermind. Hell, I can *still* cut his head off." He dropped his left hand down the left side of his saddle. When he brought it up, it clutched an ax with what looked like brown blood streaking the blade. "Just soon as I cut off yours."

Longarm had taken his reins in his left hand. Now, cutting his eyes between the two grave diggers and Dixon, he slid his right hand up toward the derringer wedged behind his waistband.

"You crazy son of a bitch," Patten said, lowering his hand from the shovel and stepping straight back, slowly lowering his own right hand toward the beat-up Colt holstered on his thigh. "You don't scare me. I ranched all over. Dealt with all kinds. Even *your* kind." He held his open hand, which shook slightly, over the Colt's worn walnut grip and swung his head back and forth, raking his graze across all four men sitting in a semicircle around him. "I warn ya, you start a fire here, you're all gonna get burned."

L.J., sitting his horse by the wagon, chuckled.

Larry smiled smugly down at Patten. His horse blew and rippled its withers.

Harlan sat his horse to Larry's far left, turned slightly toward the grave and the grave diggers. His dark eyes were nervous as he glanced between Patten and Loony Larry, waiting for a signal that he should bring his Henry rifle to bear.

Patten glanced over his shoulder at the black-bearded man standing frozen near the front of the wagon, his jaw hanging, face slack with fear. Patten returned his gaze to Dixon and stretched his lips back from his teeth as he barked tensely, "Pete, for chrissakes, pick up that barn blaster. It ain't doin' you no good leaning against the wheel!"

Pete opened and closed his mouth a couple of times. Then, keeping his eyes on the killers around him, slowly extended his left arm toward the shotgun.

"Uh-uh," L.J. said casually, dribbling a tobacco quid over his stirrup. "I wouldn't, Pete. You still gotta chance to live . . . if you promise to pull your picket pins. But if you touch that gut shredder there, I'm gonna drill one hole through your left eye. Then, before you even have time to fall, I'm gonna drill another hole through your right eye."

The black-bearded gent scrunched up his eyes. His chest rose and fell sharply, and sweat shone on his forehead. Longarm thought he would piss his pants or have a stroke.

L.J. glanced at Loony Larry, who sat on his claybank with that same, smug, cunning smile. "That's right, ain't it, Larry? I wouldn't wanna go givin' 'em no false hope. They do still have a chance to vamoose, don't they?"

No one said anything. The breeze ruffled the grass. A couple of cattle mooed. It was so quiet that Longarm, who continued inching his right hand toward his waistband, could hear the crunch of the cattle cropping grass.

Patten stared up at Dixon, the older man's face a mask of rage and terror.

Dixon grinned inside his snowy, drooping mustache.

Patten's hand dropped to his Colt's grip as he shouted, "You murderin' pile o'—"

Quickly but casually, still smiling that crazy smile, Loony Larry extended his Remington straight out over the claybank's head. At the same time, Longarm palmed the derringer, snapped the right hammer back, and jerked the peashooter up and across his saddle horn, taking quick aim on Larry's gun hand, and pulled the trigger.

The derringer hiccupped, smoke puffing up around the double, gold-plated barrels. A small, round hole appeared in the middle of Dixon's gun hand, just behind the knuckles.

Loony Larry screamed and jerked his hand up. His Colt roared.

The bullet blew up a couple of strands of Patten's hair before plopping into the mud piled behind him.

As Dixon dropped his revolver and grabbed his bloody, shaking hand, screaming at the tops of his lungs, his horse whinnied shrilly and pitched suddenly. Dixon flew straight back on the claybank's ass, but Longarm didn't see him roll off the horse's left hip because the buckskin, frightened by both the gunshot and the claybank's whinny, bucked as well, and Longarm turned forward and gripped the horse's reins in his left hand to keep from being thrown himself.

As the claybank rose off its front hooves, a rifle barked. The slug whistled over Longarm's right shoulder. The lawman peered around the lunging horse's neck. L.J. sat his horse in front of the wagon, gritting his teeth as he glared over the barrel of his Winchester carbine. As the buckskin dropped back down toward the ground, Longarm aimed the derringer at the blond rannie and fired.

L.J. had just turned the rifle to rack a fresh round into the chamber. Longarm's slug smashed into the rifle's forestock and barrel with an angry thwack, and blue sparks flew up around the barrel and into the younker's bunched face.

The kid cursed shrilly and dropped the rifle, and then Longarm threw himself out of his saddle, hitting the ground on both feet and facing the horse. He fell back from the pitching, rearing buckskin and, glancing left, saw the butt of his own rifle protruding from Dixon's jouncing saddle boot.

As the roar of a shotgun rose from the other side of the grave and a revolver popped, men yelling and horses screaming, hooves thudding and tack squawking, Longarm wrapped his left hand around the rifle's butt, gave it a jerk, then threw himself right to avoid the claybank's kicking rear hooves.

He hit the ground on a shoulder and, jacking a round into the Winchester's breech, angled the barrel upward. The rancher, Patten, stood where he'd been standing before, feet spread as he crouched and triggered his old Colt.

To Longarm's left, Loony Larry, who'd just gained his knees while clutching his bloody right hand, gave another scream and, blood flying as Patten's .44 round creased his right temple, tumbled backward in the sagebrush, his shrill, enraged screams rising even louder than before.

"Fuck!" L.J. cried, hunched forward in his saddle, his left hand clutching his right shoulder. His hat was gone

128

and his short blond hair blew around the top of his head, his neckerchief buffeting in the wind. As he gigged his horse toward Longarm, raging, he grabbed one of his silver-plated Remingtons and thumbed the hammer back.

On his back, head up, Longarm drew a bead on the kid and fired, the slug punching through the kid's right shoulder and evoking another shrill scream. Longarm fired twice more as the kid's horse bounded toward him, one slug plunking through his throat, the other through his breastbone. The lawman threw himself left, feeling the wind of the horse's scissoring hooves as the paint blew on past and headed toward the open country beyond the ranch yard.

Now chest down in the sagebrush, Longarm lifted his head, spitting grit from his teeth. The other hard case, Harlan, was exchanging gunfire with Patten about fifty yards away. Harlan was still on his horse, facing Patten, who stood sideways, his old Colt extended straight out from his right shoulder and trading lead with the Bar B gunnie before Harlan, slumped low in his saddle and gritting his teeth, reined his pinto around and heeled it off in the same direction the kid's horse had headed.

Standing statue still and rock calm, Patten triggered another shot, but the Colt's hammer clicked benignly against the firing pin.

"Shit!" he groused, lowering the Colt as Harlan dwindled into the distance, slumped low, one arm hanging straight down past his thigh, chin tipped toward his chest.

He crossed the path of the kid who, Longarm saw, had fallen out of his saddle only to have gotten one boot hung up in the stirrup. His body flopped along the ground beside the fleeing horse even as the horse splashed across the creek and mounted the buttes beyond.

Someone groaned to his right, and Longarm turned sharply. Loony Larry lay on a shoulder, facing Longarm, blood dribbling down from the deep gash on his temple. He held his bloody right hand in his left, gritting his teeth and cursing. Holding his rifle on the crazy killer, Longarm stood, walked over, grabbed the second gun from the man's holster, and tossed it into the brush.

A warm wind of relief blew through him as he stared down at the white-haired, bald-pated killer thrashing and cursing like a trapped lynx.

He had the son of a bitch, once and for all.

A woman's husky voice shouted, "Hold it right there!"

He turned to see the woman who had been standing in the doorway—big and shapeless, wearing a sweater over her dress and holding an old Sharps rifle in her hands—move toward him from the direction of the house. She lowered her head to aim down the rifle's barrel at the lawman, moving steadily to within thirty yards and closing.

The dog slunk along behind her, ears back and tail down, casting furtive looks out from behind her billowing gray dress and whining.

"One move and I'll blow a hole in you the size of a barn door, you black demon from hell!"

Chapter 13

"Shoot the son of a bitch, Maude!" the black-bearded gent called Pete shouted. He was on his knees, his shotgun broken open, frantically pinching out the spent wads he'd peppered L.J. with. "Drill him!"

The old woman stopped and stared hard at Longarm, bunching her lips as he squinted down the rusty barrel of the Sharps.

"Hold on, there, Mother!" Patten called behind Longarm. "If that hombre hadn't drilled a hole through Dixon's hand, that kill-crazy son of a bitch would have fixed me with a third eye!"

Holding the Winchester in his right hand, Longarm spread his arms as he faced the old woman and the dog peering out from behind her. "Put the rifle down, ma'am. Name's Custis Long, deputy U.S. marshal from the Third District Court in Denver. I was only riding with this son of a bitch"—he glanced at Loony Larry Dixon hunkered down on both knees while clutching his bloody right hand to his chest and glaring up at Longarm—"till I could take him down. As you can see, he's down."

The woman blinked, shuttling her suspicious gaze between Longarm and Loony Larry, moving her lips like a cow chewing cud. Finally, she lowered the rifle and glared down at Larry. "Murderin' bastard. Comin' onto my graze, threatenin' my boys, shootin' at my *dog!*"

She hacked up phlegm from her throat and spat a soupy wad onto the back of Larry's bald head. The killer jerked as though he'd been shot, then whipped toward the old woman who, wheeling, strode off toward the cabin, the brown and white dog in tow.

"She can't treat me like that, goddamnit!" Larry complained shrilly to Longarm. "If I'm your prisoner, goddamnit, you gotta see I ain't spit upon by no rotten-crotched old hag!"

The woman didn't turn around or even slow her step as he shouted shrilly at her back, "You fuckin' bitch! I'm gonna come back and kill your boys *and* your dog and then I'm gonna kill you slow . . . strangle ya with your own putrid guts!"

"That ain't no way to talk to Mother!" Patten said, running up from behind Longarm with his old Colt extended at Larry's head.

"Shoot him, Vince!" Pete called from the wagon. "Blow his fuckin' head off!"

Longarm nudged Patten aside with his hip and shoved the gun away with the barrel of his Winchester. "Hold on, goddamnit! I didn't walk through hell to bring in a carcass. I'm bringin' this man back to Denver alive, and anyone tries to send me packin' a stiff is going toe-down their ownselves!"

Levering the Winchester, he raised the rifle to his shoulder and aimed first at Patten, then at Pete, and then back again. The men stared at him hard before their faces fell slack.

Patten spat with disgust and glanced at Pete, who'd gained his feet and, standing near the back of the wagon, a bullet graze leaking blood on his left cheek, held his shotgun low at his side.

"Don't see why you wanna waste your time, Deputy, but shit, I reckon it's your time," Pete said with a cowed expression, moving forward to glare down at Dixon. "If you change your mind, though, let me know."

"'Preciate the offer," Longarm said, lowering the Winchester and looking around.

Dixon's claybank stood about a hundred yards away, grazing near the stream with its reins hanging.

He said, "What you both *can* do is hold your weapons on the kill-crazy bastard while I fetch his horse." He gave each man a steely eyed glance. "Can you do that without killing him unprovoked?"

When they'd both grunted and shrugged like chastised schoolboys and allowed they guessed they could, Longarm snorted wryly and pressed the barrel of his Winchester against Loony Larry's bald head. "Don't provoke 'em, Larry."

Longarm's buckskin hadn't fled as far as Dixon's claybank, so he first ran down the buckskin and rode over to the claybank.

The clay whinnied fearfully and trotted off a few steps, peering warily over its shoulder, but Longarm cooed and clucked and finally got the horse settled down. He tied the clay's reins to his saddle horn, then fished around in

Dixon's saddlebags to find his cartridge belt coiled around his holstered .44.

He wrapped the belt around his waist with a satisfied sigh—heeled at last!—then, adjusting the holster on his left hip and angling the walnut grip toward his belly, mounted up and trailed the clay over to where Dixon sat on the ground where Longarm had left him, wrapping his wounded hand with his neckerchief while he grunted and groaned and loudly cussed Longarm, the Pattens, God, and his own lousy luck.

The Patten brothers watched as Longarm tied the outlaw's wrists together with strips cut from the outlaw's own lariat. He ordered Dixon onto the clay's back, then tied his wrists to the saddle horn and lashed his ankles together beneath the horse's belly while Dixon cursed him and threatened to cut his ears and balls off and then to do the same to the rest of the males in his family before violating all the women.

"Seems to me you oughta just shoot the son of a bitch and throw him in the creek," Pete Patten said. "I wouldn't ride all the way to town, listenin' to that hate-spewin' son of a bitch."

"We wouldn't tell a soul," his brother said, holding the shovel across his bony shoulders. He nodded at Dixon, snarling like a rabid cougar atop the claybank. "Go ahead, do yourself a favor, Deputy. No man should have to listen to that sorta talk. I mean, he's involvin' your mother and grandmother now."

Longarm chuckled, remembering the dwarf he had locked up in the Snakehead Gap jailhouse. "I'm right used to it." He glanced in the direction the kid, L.J., had been dragged. "If you come upon the kid's horse out there, he's yours. As far as the kid himself, you can bury him or not. I doubt anyone'll come lookin' for him, and it makes no difference to me."

"We could use that horse," Pete Patten allowed, leaning on his shotgun and staring toward the buttes.

"What about them crazy girls?" his brother asked Longarm. "They got more gunnies than just him and them other two."

"Locking up ole Larry should take some of the starch out of their bloomers." Longarm strode over and picked up the funnel-brimmed hat Harlan had left lying on the other side of the freshly dug grave. He batted the hat against his thigh, inspected it, plucked a weed from the band, and set it on his head.

Mounting the buckskin, he sighed and stared back in the direction of the Bar B headquarters, an uneasy feeling prickling at his nether regions. "But I'll no doubt be back." He pinched his hat brim to the Patten brothers, then glanced at Dixon sitting the claybank behind him, blood showing through the neckerchief wrapped around his hand.

"Ready, Larry?"

"Ready?" Loony Larry said, blinking beneath the brim of his bullet-crowned hat and shoving his face forward. "I'm ready for your sister. The first one couldn't suck for shit. If the other can't, I'm gonna tie her tongue around my neck and wear it for a charm."

"Jesus," Pete Patten said, dabbing at his bullet-burned cheek. "That's about as foul a son of a bitch as I ever heard. You better not let him get away from you."

"You do," his brother warned, shaking his head and whistling, his wary blue eyes on Dixon, "there'll be hell to pave and no hot pitch!"

"He'll cut your damn head off, sure enough," Pete speculated grimly.

"Don't worry," Longarm said, urging the buckskin ahead and jerking the claybank along behind him. "Till I get him back to Denver, he won't be leaving my sight to take so much as a green shit."

With that, he booted the buckskin into a trot, and the claybank followed suit, nickering and twitching its ears as it trotted just off the buckskin's right hip.

"Knew I shoulda shot you last night," Loony Larry grumbled. "But don't worry, you sow-screwin' lawdog, I got me a feelin' I'll get a second chance."

"Don't count on it," Longarm growled as he put the horses into the stream.

"Don't *you* count on it, old son," Dixon laughed as the horses gained the opposite bank. "And don't count on keepin' that hat for long, neither." He laughed again, throwing his head back on his shoulders as the horses climbed a trough between the chalky, muddy buttes. " 'Cause you ain't gonna have anything to *set it on* for long!"

Loony Larry continued laughing hysterically and sending occasional wolflike yowls skyward as the horses gained the tableland above the buttes. Longarm turned the buckskin and stopped just off Loony Larry's left stirrup. He drew his rifle from its saddle boot and laid it across his thighs.

"What're you doin'?" Larry said, tears of laughter streaming down his cheeks.

Longarm raised the rifle in one hand and rammed the butt against Larry's left cheekbone. The man screamed and sagged back in his saddle, his eyes rolling back in his head as a red welt rose on his cheek and he fell into semiconsciousness, only his tied hands keeping him mounted.

"There now," Longarm said, turning the buckskin ahead as he sheathed the rifle. "That's better."

In refreshing silence, he rode west across the rolling, drying prairie, leading the claybank upon which Loony Larry swayed in his saddle, now and then giving a groan or anguished grunt. Longarm rode as fast as he dared push the two horses through prairie dog country made even more treacherous with recently flooded washes and quicksand pools.

He wasn't sure how badly Harlan had been wounded at the Patten ranch, but if the man made it back to the Diamond Bar B with news of Larry's capture, the girls would, without a doubt, send riders to intercept Longarm before he could get their prized stud and gunslick locked up in the Snakehead Gap jailhouse.

He wasn't sure where he was, but he figured town lay a good three or four hours northwest, which meant that if he didn't split the wind, the gun-hung gals of the Bar B ranch would have time to set a trap for him.

He had a feeling they could set a good one.

After forty-five minutes of solid riding, he stopped in the shade beneath a lone cottonwood to check Larry's wounded hand. There wasn't much point going to all this work if the man was going to bleed to death. Larry had regained consciousness, but having decided he was better off being seen and not heard, only muttered curses under his breath as Longarm inspected the wound.

Blood had sopped the neckerchief tied around it, but it was starting to congeal. The outlaw would probably last until Longarm could get him to town and find a sawbones.

Tightening the neckerchief until Larry hissed sharply

through his teeth, Longarm mounted back up, gigged the buckskin ahead, and resumed angling northwest toward a jog of hills he'd noted when he'd left town the day before.

The hills didn't look far away, but it wasn't until three hours later that the land began rising and pitching around him, cut by deep, narrow draws still wet from floodwater and strewn with fresh debris. It was with some trepidation and with his Winchester resting across his saddlebows that he entered a muddy canyon with steep clay walls and floury white buttes rising on both sides.

Mud swallows swooped, flashing like bits of steel in the angling sunlight.

Loony Larry chuckled. Longarm glanced at the outlaw. "You want another tattoo?"

"I'm behavin'," Larry said innocently. "I sense you might be a little nervous. I know I would be. This is a prime spot for an ambush. Sure is."

When Longarm had turned forward, a roaring, wolflike howl rose, echoing off the canyon walls and setting Longarm's heart to leaping. Gritting his teeth, he hipped around in his saddle.

The outlaw sat grinning through his snow-white mustache, pale blue eyes slitted beneath his hat brim. Longarm turned the buckskin back toward the claybank and began lifting his rifle butt.

"I'll be quiet," Larry said with false chagrin, leaning back in his saddle.

"Yeah, you wi—" Longarm stopped suddenly. The butte behind him cast a shadow across the sunlit bank before him, over Loony Larry's left shoulder. Atop the butte shadow, the shadow of a hat and rifle barrel moved.

Longarm threw himself out of his saddle. He hadn't hit the ground before the shot smashed across the narrow canyon like a whiplash.

Chapter 14

As Larry loosed another echoing howl and the horses whinnied and pitched, Longarm rolled onto his back and raised the Winchester toward the bluff behind him. Aiming quickly at the shooter peering over the conical peak, and finding his smoking Sharps still aimed at Longarm, the lawman fired three quick rounds—*boom-rasp, boom-rasp, boom!*

The man screamed and sagged forward, dropping the rifle. As man and gun rolled down the bluff, the buckskin tore up canyon, nickering and buck-kicking. The claybank followed, Loony Larry laughing and yowling and shouting: "Get him, boys! Get him, girls! Come one, come all to the shootin' match!"

His voice dwindled as the horses plunged around a bend. Longarm ejected a smoking shell casing, looking around wildly as another head and rifle appeared over another conical peak on the same side of the canyon as the first.

KA-BOOM!

Smoke puffed around the rifle's large, round maw as the heavy-caliber slug slammed into the damp sand and gravel about four inches to the right of Longarm's bent knee. Longarm scrambled to his feet and sprinted across the canyon floor.

Holding the Winchester in one hand, he heeled it up the canyon wall as the man he'd shot tumbled down the slope to his right. As shooter and rifle rolled on past, Longarm caught a glimpse of the round, flat face of the man called Moose.

The lawman continued climbing, grabbing at shrubs and rocks and hearing the thud of Moose hitting the canyon floor behind him. The shooter on the other bluff crest took a couple more shots, but both slugs spanged off rocks or chewed up sand at Longarm's heels. Then the lawman slipped around the left side of the butte, putting the butte between him and the second bushwhacker.

He climbed the notch between buttes, then slipped around the backside of the one from which Moose had tried to drill him. He stole around the butte's backside about ten feet below the crest, moving toward the bluff from which the second gunman had fired.

When the other butte top edged into view, he stopped and dropped to a knee, holding the rifle barrel up in his right hand.

He could see the place where the second bushwhacker had propped himself, but the man was no longer there. Sand and gravel trickled down the side of the butte. A half second later, down slope, a head slipped out from behind a boulder, near the trough between the two bluffs. A rifle barrel flashed in the sunlight.

Longarm dropped the Winchester's forestock to his left hand and triggered four quick shots, the blasts booming off the slopes and boulders around him.

The second bushwhacker screamed, stumbled back,

and dropped his Sharps Big Fifty, a startled expression on his face. It was the man called Lyle, who'd been sitting in front of last night's parlor fire with Cassie. His white, high-crowned hat tumbled off his shoulder as he took another step straight back, chaps flapping about his black denim–clad legs, spurs chinging on the rocks. He raised his hands to the several blood-spraying holes in his chest as another glistened on the nub of his left cheek, dribbling blood into his chestnut mustache.

Damn, Longarm thought, staring at the man's walleyed face, from which the life was quickly leeching. That's Lyle "Walleye" Petersen from up in Dakota. Longarm had been too preoccupied with Loony Larry last night to recognize the regulator who, if the lawman remembered the paper on the man, was wanted in nearly every state in the West and even in a few back East.

A brutal gun for hire.

Those girls hired nothing but the best. Or worst, depending on how you looked at it.

As Petersen sagged back against the far bluff wall, using his hands to cushion his fall, as though he were just sitting down for a blow, Longarm scrambled down the slope. The man stared up as Longarm stood over him.

"Walleye," Longarm said, pinching his hat brim. "It's been a privilege to trim your wick, you son of a bitch. I don't suppose you'd wanna tell me how many more are out here, would you?"

The man's lips moved, pink tongue sliding around behind them like a mouse peering out of its hole. His throat worked and he made gurgling sounds as he tried to spit. Finally, he gave up and died, tumbling sideways onto the rocks, which he promptly smeared with blood.

"Much obliged," Longarm grunted, then began moving carefully through the crease between buttes toward the canyon.

Scouring the area with his gaze, holding his cocked rifle high and ready, Longarm stole back to the canyon floor. Neither seeing nor hearing anything but the late afternoon breeze sifting amongst the rocks and the swallows chirping in protest of all the recent commotion, he moved up the canyon floor, following the fresh prints of his and Loony Larry's horses.

Ahead, a doe and a fawn trotted out of an offshooting arm of the canyon. They started toward Longarm, but when their eyes found him, wheeled as one and sprinted off in the other direction, white tails raised as their hooves clattered on the rocky ground.

Longarm crept over to the left wall of the canyon and moved slowly forward, careful not to kick any rocks and give himself away. When he came to the offshooting arm, he paused, pricking his ears to listen, then turned quickly into the ten-foot gap and stared up a rock- and brush-choked trough between crumbling butte slopes. Wanda Diamond was leading a black, blaze-faced mare toward him through the trough, the mare's reins in one hand, a Winchester carbine in the other. Wanda had lifted her chin to peer around the sloping butte walls above.

The black's right front hoof kicked a stone down the incline, and Wanda dropped her gaze toward Longarm. She stopped abruptly with a surprised grunt, eyes widening, her lower jaw dropping suddenly.

The lawman spread his feet and extended his Winchester straight out from his right hip, the barrel aimed at the girl's ample bosom rising and falling behind a sweat-damp calico shirt buttoned low enough to reveal an alluring sweep of

144

cleavage. Her man's Stetson shaded the top half of her tan, oval face. Over her blue denims she wore black bull-hide chaps trimmed with silver conchos. Two Colts, one positioned for the cross-draw, jutted from holsters on her thighs.

For stretched seconds, neither of them said anything. Longarm kept his ears pricked for more sounds where she'd come from. He glanced at the carbine she carried by its forestock and wagged his own Winchester at her.

"Chuck it off to your right."

She stared at him, her full mouth quirked in an annoying grin. Finally, she threw the carbine into the rocks and brush along the trough.

"Now the gun belt."

She sighed but maintained the grin. Unbuckling the cartridge belt, she tossed the belt and holsters into the brush with the carbine.

"My sister is so angry at you!" Wanda pursed her lips. "Aubrey thinks the sun rises and sets on Larry. Where you plan on takin' him?"

"He broke prison in Montana Territory, but he'll probably hang in Denver for his sundry crimes, not the least of which is killin' the badge toters from Snakehead Gap."

"He was right. You are a lawdog." Wanda chuckled. "You had me fooled. Most o' them are noodle-dicked."

Longarm started toward her, swinging his head around to glance behind and then up the slope behind Wanda and the mare. "How's Harlan?"

"Dead."

Longarm stopped in front of the beautiful girl, her copper hair hanging straight down from her hat, a few strands tickling her cleavage.

She shook her hair back from her eyes and looked up at him, squinting. "You mind telling me your real name?"

"Custis Long. Deputy U.S. Marshal out of Denver."

Wanda looked shocked. "The one they call Longarm?"

"Stay here." Keeping the Winchester leveled on her, he moved around her and the horse as he climbed the trough in the direction from which they'd come.

At the top of the rise, he looked around at the backsides of the chalky buttes banded with iron and coal, then out at the rolling rangeland beyond, which was cut with gullies, here and there pushing up a lone, scrubby willow or cottonwood. Except for the breeze-ruffled grass, nothing moved.

He glanced at Wanda. "Where are your sisters and your other men?"

"Covering another route north," she said cockily.

Longarm stretched his gaze northward once more. Satisfied he was alone, he started back toward Wanda, and stopped abruptly. She'd opened her shirt, exposing her full, round breasts. Holding the flaps of her shirt back with the fists on her hips, she cocked one foot and canted a head coquettishly.

"How 'bout one more for the road?"

Longarm had to admit to a prick of desire, but he chuckled dryly. "So you can grab a gun and shoot my guts out my backbone?"

"Come on," Wanda said. "I'll behave . . . do whatever you want." She glanced at a shady spot at the base of the slope to her right. "You won't regret it."

"What I have a feelin' I *will* regret is not taking you in. But for the moment, I have my hands full." Longarm squinted his right eye and aimed his rifle at her one-handed, his craggy features flushing with anger. "You get your pretty tits back to your ranch and start minding your manners. Get rid of any gunmen you got left and throw

146

an olive branch to your neighbors. Any more trouble from you and your sisters, and you'll all hang."

With that he stomped past her, picked up her gun belt, and tossed it over his shoulder. He picked up her rifle and, keeping the bare-breasted girl in the periphery of his vision, continued on down the trough between the buttes.

At the intersection with the main canyon, he turned around to face her. She stood by the mare. She hadn't covered her breasts yet, but she looked more frustrated now than saucy, hands hanging straight down her sides, lips pursed.

Longarm pinched his hatbrim to her, then moved out into the main canyon and began heeling it in the direction that his and Larry's horses had galloped. He paused to toss the girl's weapons into a snag of brush and rocks, then resumed his trek down canyon.

He found the horses and Larry about a hundred yards down the canyon, in a thin stand of willows flanking a muddy stream. Dixon had somehow managed to free his hands and his right boot, but his left boot remained in its stirrup. Sitting on the ground beside the claybank, which was idly drawing water from the stream, Dixon was reaching forward and grunting and cursing as he tried to free his left boot tied up before him. His hat was gone, and his pink pate shone in the sun like a freshly plucked chicken, his cottony hair sliding around in the breeze.

Hearing Longarm's footsteps, he dropped his hands from the stirrup and turned his sweaty face to peer over his shoulder. He bunched his lips with fury.

"Shit!"

He flopped back on the ground, breathing hard. He looked like he was about to cry.

Longarm stared down at him, his long shadow falling

across the killer's supine, rough-garbed frame. "What are you tryin' to do, Larry? Cheat the hangman?"

"When I kill you, lawdog"—Loony Larry brushed a tear of frustration from his cheek with the heel of his right hand—"they're gonna hear you yellin' all the way to Mexico."

Longarm tattooed the killer's forehead with his Winchester's butt, sending Loony Larry to the edge of unconsciousness once more. Then he back-and-bellied the groaning heap back onto the claybank, tied him up tight, and set off for Snakehead Gap once again.

Chapter 15

Longarm and Loony Larry Dixon pulled into Snakehead Gap in the late afternoon as the sun angled behind the Rockies unseen in the west and flooded the town's main drag with purple shadows stitched with falling cotton-wood seeds.

The street was all but deserted. A couple of yellow pups chewed on each other's necks in front of the women's hat shop while saddled horses slumped before the town's three saloons and a stocky boy sitting on the step before the mercantile prodded the dirt before him with a carved-wooden rifle, a coonskin cap tipped back off his sandy blond head.

The long ride with a hole in his hand and two bruises in the shape of a brass-plated rifle butt adorning his cheek and forehead had kept Loony Larry in a relatively peace-ful slumber. As Larry leaned back in his saddle, secured by his hands and feet to the claybank, quietly grumbling, Longarm drew the horses up before the boy in the coon-skin cap.

"Why so long-faced, sonny? Kill off all the Injuns too early, did you?" Longarm smiled at his joke.

The kid looked at him with a bored air, prodding the dust with the end of his toy rifle and saying nothing.

Longarm let the grin die on his lips. Kids had no sense of humor these days. "How 'bout you take these horses over to the livery barn by the hotel for me? Tell the hostlers to give 'em the works."

The kid hiked a shoulder and glanced absently up the street, where a piano tinkled faintly. "A man's gotta make a livin', mister."

Longarm plucked a coin from his jeans pocket and flipped it to the kid, who caught it against his chest. He looked down at it, frowning as though he'd been tossed a turd. Flipping the coin in his hand and glancing up the street as before, he said, "Price of rock candy's gone up in these parts, mister. Same for chocolate and jelly beans."

Longarm muttered a curse and plucked another coin from his jeans pocket. "That oughta buy you a whole bag of rock candy, chocolate, *and* jelly beans, sonny, and I reckon you got a future in snake oil!"

The kid glanced down at the silver dollar. His eyes brightened but when he looked up at Longarm again, he carefully arranged a casual expression. "That'll do. The hotel, you say?"

"The hotel," Longarm said, swinging the buckskin toward the stone jailhouse slumped on the other side of the street, shaded by the two-story harness shop beside it. "And roust a sawbones. I need him over at the jailhouse pronto."

He pulled his horse and the claybank up to the hitch rack and swung down from the saddle. The pudgy boy came up, toy gun resting on his shoulder, and grabbed the reins of both horses while staring up at Loony Larry. The outlaw seemed to be coming out of his stupor, blinking his pain-spoked eyes and smacking his lips.

The kid glanced at Longarm. "Is that . . . is that . . ."

"The ring-tailed devil known as Loony Larry Dixon?" Longarm nodded as he cut the killer's wrists free of his saddle horn with a Barlow knife. "You got it, junior."

"Holy shit!" the kid cried as, barely before Longarm had the grumbling Dixon out of his saddle and his rifle out of its saddle sheath, he ran off up the street, jerking both horses along behind him and turning disbelieving glances over his shoulder.

Longarm prodded Loony Larry up to the jailhouse's timbered door. "Open it," he said.

Coming out of his stupor, Larry shook his head and told Longarm to fuck himself. Longarm pressed the rifle barrel against the back of the killer's head and thumbed back the trigger with a loud, ratcheting sound.

Larry chuffed angrily, tripped the latch, and moved inside. Longarm followed, keeping the rifle aimed at the back of the man's head, and peered into the shadows of the musty room, his gaze moving to the desk a few feet from the door as the man who'd been sitting there, boots crossed on the desktop, sat up suddenly, making the swivel rocker squawk sharply.

"Hello, Marshal!" It was the man Vernon Wade had been shaving when Longarm had first ridden into town, Jack Doyle. "Have to say, I didn't expect you back so soon!"

"Feels like about three long months to me," Longarm said, prodding Loony Larry toward the three cells lined up at the back of the room. He grabbed the key ring off the nail in the building's center post and, keeping the rifle snugged up against the crazy killer, rammed the key in the lock, twisted and turned it until the rusty bolt clicked, then hazed Larry inside.

The man was so worn out and beaten up that he sank instantly down on the cell's sole cot. "Home again, home again, jumpety-bum-and-the-schoolmarm's-diddlin'-the preacher's-son!" he sang, looking around dully and grinning. "I gotta tell you, Marshal, I sure never thought I'd meet up with a man who could put me back in one of these things." He shook his head tiredly, chin grazing his chest. "No, sir, I never seen this one comin'. Don't take it personal that I hope you die hard."

From the shadows of the cell to the left of Loony Larry's, a high, raspy voice said, "Who the hell's this big pile of yellow goat shit?"

With all that had happened in the past twenty-four hours, Longarm had forgotten about the dwarf—Tim Turley, the evil Titus Turley's just as evil twin. But now he saw the little creature standing there in his cell, facing Loony Larry through the bars, his large, bright eyes bulging as they moved sharply around in their sockets, sizing up his fellow prisoner.

Larry glowered back at him, a slow smile growing on the crazy killer's mustached lips. It was like watching a couple of curs sniffing each other's asses to see which one had had the better prowl the night before.

"Who the hell is this?" Larry chuckled as he dropped his chin to indicate the dwarf. "Looks like a damn rat that ate so much shit he got too big for the privy!" Larry laughed.

Tim Turley wrapped his fat, stubby fingers around the bars and shoved his warty, pockmarked face between them, firing daggers of pure venom from his eyes. "Hey, albino boy, you like the smell of shit so much, squat down here and lick my ass! Then buff my balls with that purty, snowy white mustache!"

Larry couldn't have been too tired, because he sprang

off his cot like a Brahma bull bolting from a rodeo chute. Thrusting both hands through the bars, he nearly snagged the dwarf by his neck before Turley leapt straight back with a mocking whoop and jumped up onto his cot and bent forward at the waist, fists on his hips, making lewd gestures with his long pink tongue.

While the verbal skirmish continued in low, menacing tones, with an exchange of mocking chuckles, Longarm turned to Jack Doyle, who stood beside his desk as though fearful of getting too close to the cells in which the man-animals were joisting.

"Never mind them," Longarm said, stretching a kink from his neck and yawning. "If we're lucky, they'll kill each other before the night's over."

Doyle stared into the cell in which Larry hunkered low, threatening the dwarf. He nodded. "That's Loony Larry Dixon, all right. Seen him myself in town one day, with two o' the girls. Came for whiskey and supplies and frilly underwear."

Longarm had just seen the five-pointed star pinned to the man's wool vest when Doyle turned to him, followed his gaze, and pulled the vest away from his chest, flushing as he showed off the star. "How's it look, Marshal? I'm the new sheriff o' Hatchet Woman County."

When Longarm only frowned at him, Doyle flushed again and hiked a shoulder. "The town council had a meetin' last night, convinced me to take the job since no one else wanted it. Vernon Wade, who's the mayor in addition to the barber and undertaker, reminded me that it'd mean an extra thirty dollars in my pocket each month. And my harness shop"—he jerked a plump, pink thumb to indicate the two-story building just east of the jailhouse—"is right handy."

Longarm scrutinized the man. He had a hard time imagining the portly Doyle leaping into the saddle to gallop after bank robbers, or swapping lead with pistoleros intent on terrorizing the town and raping all its women. But in his years prowling the tall and uncut, he'd seen less capable men toting tin badges on their chests.

"Congratulations, Doyle," he said, extending his hand to the man.

"Appreciate it, Marshal."

"Since you're all official and all, you mind holdin' down the fort and keepin' an eye on these two while I rustle up a meal? I sent a kid for a doctor to sew up Larry's hand. Make sure he does it through the bars and that Larry doesn't get his hand on any sharp objects."

"You got it," the portly man said, hitching his old cap-and-ball revolver up higher on his hip with a self-important air. "Hell, why don't you get yourself a meal and a couple drinks and a few hours of shut-eye? I'll watch over Loony Larry and the dwarf until you're ready to haul both their asses to Denver."

"I might take you up on a meal and a nap." Longarm went to the door and peered west, into the darkening countryside from which he and Loony had traveled. "But I'll be back in a couple of hours to spell you. I *think* I either snuffed out or at least *discouraged* the Diamond girls and the rest of their cold-steel artists, but I can't be sure. One of us best keep watch till morning."

He glanced back to where the dwarf and Loony Larry were still going at it like a couple of bobcats in separate cages. "I'll eat, wash up, take a snooze in a proper bed, and be back here before ten o'clock. You have any trouble, squeeze off three quick shots."

"All right," Doyle said. "I'll yell over to Vernon's place,

have Olga rustle up some grub for the prisoners." He glanced into the cells where Loony Larry and Tim Turley were still exchanging threats and insults through the bars, the dwarf grabbing his crotch and jumping up and down just out of reach of Larry's flailing hands. "Maybe once they smell food, they'll settle down."

"I wouldn't count on it." Longarm pinched his hat brim to the new sheriff. "Later."

Shouldering his rifle, he went out and once more peered back the way he'd come. The night was closing down quickly, with several stars kindling in the lilac eastern sky. A couple of coyotes howled. Spying no movement except for a single rider—an old man in ragged ranch garb astride a swaybacked gray mule—heading in from the countryside and no doubt making a beeline for a drink, Longarm turned and headed east along the main drag.

Heading in the general direction of the hotel, he stopped at the first cafe he stumbled upon and sat down to a hearty helping of antelope roast and potatoes smothered in rich, charred gravy. He followed it up with peach cobbler, and, for no extra charge, the half-breed who ran the place treated him to coffee laced with the hooch he brewed out back, which wasn't bad for these parts. Longarm appreciated the drink, for he'd lost his bottle of Maryland rye along with the rest of his possibles in the flooded ravine.

The panther sweat hadn't been harsh going down, but it must have been nearly pure alcohol, for Longarm found himself stumbling down the side street on which the hotel was located and feeling as though his tired, battered bones were dissolving beneath his skin.

The hotel's proprietor, Wilfred Ramsay, wasn't happy

to see him after the commotion around the privy two nights ago, but he twirled the register and pen toward the ragged-looking lawman, anyway.

"I'll only be here a couple of hours," Longarm told Ramsay through a wide yawn. "If I sleep past ten, knock on my door, will you?"

He tossed an extra coin down on the register then, leaving Ramsay grumbling behind him, and headed upstairs to the same room he'd had before. After a whore's bath at the washstand, he stripped down to his birthday suit, blew out the lamp on the dresser, and collapsed rather than rolled into bed. He'd barely shut his eyes before sleep claimed him, heavy and thick as a tub of warm tar.

When he opened his eyes again, he froze, staring straight up at the ceiling, his lower jaw dropping slowly, anxious lines spoking his eyes. Through a thin veil of misty light, he could make out each of the wainscoting's narrow, knotted slats.

At first he thought there must be a full moon, but then he turned to the window. The sky beyond the drawn, lemon yellow curtains was pearling with the soft light of dawn.

"Shit!" Longarm barked, throwing the covers back and swinging his feet to the floor. He grabbed his old Ingersoll off the nightstand and flipped the lid.

Christ almighty, it was 5:10 in the morning!

He cursed again, hauled his tired body up from the bed, and stomped around the room, cursing and dressing and wondering why Ramsay hadn't woken him. When he'd stomped into his boots and donned Harlan's hat, he stalked downstairs to find Wilfred Ramsay sound asleep in a rocking chair between the hotel's front door and a dusty, potted palm.

The man held an illustrated magazine open on his lap.

His chin was tipped to his chest, feet propped on a foot-stool, and his snores resounded around the room, rattling the lamps and window panes.

Ramsay didn't stir as Longarm, muttering angrily, tramped past the man. Shouldering his rifle, he headed up the side street toward the main drag.

At the side street's intersection with Main, he paused at the corner of a tobacco shop and looked around. A fresh breeze funneled down the street, making a couple of shingle chains squawk, and morning birds chirped in the prairie surrounding the town. A small animal, either a fox or a coyote, was nosing around trash in the street about one block west.

Otherwise, nothing moved. No unnatural sounds. And nothing looked amiss.

Funny, though, that Doyle hadn't sent someone to fetch Longarm from the hotel. He might have just de-cided to let Longarm sleep. If there'd been trouble, the lawman no doubt would have heard gunfire.

He continued east along the boardwalks, staying to the shadows of the building fronts and keeping his eyes peeled. Ahead, he saw the squat, stone jailhouse, the front wall concealed by the darkness under the brush arbor.

As he came within forty yards, he slowed his pace. No lamplight emanated from either of the building's two front windows.

Would Doyle have gone to sleep without fetching Longarm first? The man was new at the job, but it didn't seem likely. Not with Loony Larry in his cell block.

Longarm paused on the boardwalk before Doyle's har-ness shop and, holding his rifle in both hands across his chest, studied the jailhouse, pricking his ears. Quietly lev-ering a fresh round into the Winchester's breech, he stepped

157

off the boardwalk and crossed the street, watching the front door push out from the jailhouse's front wall between the two dark windows.

A rising breeze swirled dust and jostled paper trash in the gap between the two buildings.

Longarm moved under the jailhouse's brush arbor, heading for the door. He stopped and listened through the door's heavy timbers. Silence. He was shoving his left hand toward the latch when something nudged his back.

With a startled grunt, Longarm swung around, bringing up the rifle. He frowned beneath the brim of Harlan's hat, and his heart turned a somersault in his chest.

Something hung from a stout beam of the brush arbor, on a rope that creaked softly in the rising breeze.

Not something.

Someone.

The dwarf.

Chapter 16

Longarm backed up against the jail's front door, holding his rifle out and whipping his head around anxiously.

Spying no movement anywhere, he returned his gaze to the dwarf hanging from an arbor beam, neck stretched a good six inches, chin dipped to his chest. As the small, lumpy body turned gently in the dawn breeze, the dwarf's face angled toward Longarm, mean little eyes glassily glaring, tongue drooping down over his thick lower lip, cheeks balled with rage and horror.

He was wearing only one of his little red boots. He must have kicked the other one off; it lay on the sunken ground beneath the arbor.

Longarm looked around once more. Then, keeping his back to the door and fumbling with the latch, shoved the door open and wheeled inside. Spreading his feet and aiming his Winchester straight out from his hip, he raked his gaze quickly back and forth across the dawn-foggy room.

At the rear, both cell doors stood open. Not surprising. Nor was Longarm surprised to see that Jack Doyle had gone the way of the dwarf, kicked back in the swivel chair behind the desk.

The newbie sheriff hadn't been hung, however. Someone had driven a hatchet through the crown of his skull. He sat in the chair, mouth drawn as though in an eternal, silent scream, staring up at the hickory ax handle angling out over his broad, fleshy, cleanly shaven face streaked with blood and brain matter, which had dribbled down from the giant gash in his head.

The building was small enough that it took only one more quick, raking glance to see that Doyle was the only man in the room. Loony Larry was gone. Probably sprung by his gun-hung wife, Aubrey, and her three sisters, including Wanda, and maybe another male gunslick or two if there were any still kicking.

Longarm moved back to the open door and, standing in the doorway, looked around the dwarf and into the street.

Were they still in town or had they headed back out to the Bar B?

As if in answer to his question, the front door of Vernon Wade's barbershop–undertaking parlor opened suddenly with a click and a screech of squeaky hinges. Wade appeared in the doorway, a night sock on his head, staring across the deserted street toward Longarm.

"Look out, Marshal!"

Something moved behind the man's head. With a shrill cry, Wade flew headfirst onto the boardwalk before the shop. A man appeared in the doorway behind him, raising a Winchester to his shoulder. Loony Larry Dixon gripped the gun with his white-bandaged right hand, and his porcelain mustache glowed in the misty light as he lowered his bald head and squinted down the barrel.

Longarm ducked and threw himself right as Loony Larry's slug careened past the dwarf to slam into the door frame with a deafening *thwhack*. The rifle's belch echoed around the street, rending the morning quiet as Longarm snaked his Winchester through the door frame, aiming around the dwarf's hanging corpse toward Vernon Wade's wood-frame business.

Loony Larry stood just inside the front door, levering a fresh shell into his Winchester. Raising his own rifle to his shoulder, Longarm got a quick glimpse of two more shooters lifting their heads above the stock troughs fronting Wade's building and yet two more peering over the lip of the building's shake-shingled roof, angling rifles toward the jailhouse.

He saw all four shooters only in the periphery of his vision, as he kept his main focus on Loony Larry, but he was certain, from the long hair falling from their men's hats and from the delicate, angular curves of their silhouetted faces, that all four were women.

Howard Diamond's lovely, gun-hung, kill-crazy daughters had come to town to break Loony Larry out of jail.

Larry himself had probably hanged the dwarf, but Longarm wondered which of the girls had chunked the ax through Jack Doyle's forehead.

He didn't have time to wonder long, nor did he have time to snap off his own shot, for all four of the girls' rifles as well as Loony Larry's roared at nearly the same time. Longarm pulled his rifle inside and rolled back against the stone wall, wincing as the five slugs hammered the wall's other side and shattered the glass in the two windows on either side of him.

As the cannonade died, the echoes of the shots chasing each other up and down the street, Longarm snaked his Winchester once more through the door frame and snapped off a shot at Loony Larry, but not before the killer had stepped back behind his own door frame.

Longarm's slug careened through the doorway to shatter glass somewhere in the barbershop's shadowy interior.

The rasping of cocking levers sounded clearly in the cool, quiet air. Longarm pulled back behind the stone wall once more as another cannonade exploded across the street. The shots peppered the wall with lead, and more slugs buzzed through the windows and open doorway to spang and spark off the wood stove behind the sheriff's desk and to chew slivers from a ceiling joist.

Longarm snapped off two quick shots through the doorway, around the dwarf's dangling corpse, then reached over to grab the door handle. He slammed the door closed as a continuous assault of flying lead hammered away at the front of the jailhouse, thumping into the stout wood door and buffeting dust from the cracks between the timbers.

Wincing as slugs whined through the windows, Longarm duck-crawled under the room's right window, crunching glass beneath his boots, and then straightened on its far side. Doffing Harlan's hat and stretching his lips back from his teeth, he edged a look around the bullet-shredded frame. From this angle he could see one of the female shooters on the roof across the street, another hunkered behind the stock trough to the left of the front door.

He waited for a lull in the shooting—there was no pause longer than two seconds—and snapped a couple of shots at the girl on the roof and three more at the stock trough. The most damage he did was to blow the hat off the girl behind the stock trough and evoke a shrill curse.

He pulled back behind the window as bullets tore into the casing and whipped through the opening to bark and spark off the cells' iron bars. A couple ricochets slammed into the side wall to his left.

He looked around. The building was about twenty feet

wide by forty feet long. And there was no back door. No way out except through the front.

Someone across the street must have been sharing the same thought. A sharp whistle rose above the rifle fire, and the firing petered to a stop.

In the heavy, ensuing silence, Loony Larry called, "Hey, Longarm, you might as well come on out of there. There ain't no way out but the front, and we'll just burn you out if you don't come hither and straightaway, old son!" Larry laughed loudly as though at the funniest joke he'd ever heard.

The laugh died to silence. A pause.

Longarm looked around the office again and rubbed his jaw. Two old rifles stood behind a rusty chain in the gun rack on the opposite wall. If he looked around, he could probably find a box or two of extra cartridges. But even if he found an entire case of .44 shells, he couldn't hole up in here for long.

He would run out of firepower and Loony Larry and the just-as-crazy Diamond girls would send him the way of the dwarf and Jack Doyle, no doubt more slowly.

They'd probably chop his head off and send it to Billy Vaile.

Longarm had an image of Billy opening a wooden packing box one sunny Denver morning while enjoying his first cup of java in his cluttered office, to find Longarm's face scowling up at him from a bloody nest of crumpled newspapers.

"Come on out, Custis," Wanda yelled from behind one of the stock troughs. "You don't wanna die in there like a mouse in its hole. You're too much man for that!"

One of the girls on the roof laughed and yelled down, "I reckon you'd know, Wanda!"

More laughter.

Longarm thumbed cartridges from his shell belt into the Winchester's loading gate. Then on hands and knees, he crawled back past the desk to the rear of the room.

Larry shouted, "Come on, Longarm, make a run for it. You might make it . . . if you run fast enough!"

As Larry howled and the women chuckled, Longarm crawled into the cell the dwarf had occupied. He set his rifle on the cot, then stood, moved to the cell's single window, and tested the four vertical bars. All were solid.

Shit.

Larry and the women continued jeering and inviting Longarm to show himself as the lawman grabbed his rifle off the cot, dropped to his hands and knees, and keeping his head below the level of the two front windows, crawled out of the dwarf's cell and into the one Larry had occupied.

Outside, a rifle barked. The slug whistled through one of the front windows and hammered a bar of the cell Longarm was in, setting his ears to ringing. He flinched.

As Larry laughed his high-pitched, mocking laugh, Longarm cursed and leaned his rifle against the cell's back wall. Casting a cautious glance behind him, he straightened quickly and tested the bars of the cell's single window.

They, too, were solid.

"Son of a *bitch* . . ." Longarm grunted, giving the last bar a frustrated jerk.

Outside, someone triggered two rifle shots into the stout, timbered door, jostling the door in its frame and sending dust sifting down from the beams over the frame.

"Come out, come out," one of the girls sang. "Don't hide away and pout!"

Another slug tore through a window, skidded off the

top off the desk, and sparked off a cell bar, setting Long-arm's ears to ringing once more. He dropped to his knees and began to turn back toward his rifle when he stopped suddenly and turned back to the wall beneath the barred window.

As the rifle fire began again sporadically, drowning the hoots and hollers of the girls and Loony Larry, Longarm hunkered low and canted his head to inspect the wall closely, running his fingers along a curving, jagged line of mortar that appeared much newer than the rest. It traced a circle around six or seven rocks, which, not as faded and soot-stained as the rest, had obviously been set within the past few years, probably to replace those knocked out by an escaping prisoner.

By a cursory inspection, it looked as though the mortar hadn't quite set. With enough force, it might be chipped away from the cracks.

Flinching and ducking as several shots hammered the bars and walls around him, his heart pumping anxiously, he pulled his Barlow knife from his pocket and began chipping away at the relatively fresh mortar with the blade's curved tip.

After a couple of hard taps that dislodged some of the brittle chinking, Longarm's heartbeat increased even more. He'd been right—the cement was cracking up, pulling away from the edges of the replacement stones. If he'd had a hammer and chisel, he'd have been out of there in no time.

But he had no hammer, no chisel, and it was only a matter of time before one of the bullets buzzing around his head found its mark.

Wincing as a ricocheting slug peppered his face with stone shards, Longarm quickly slipped his revolver from its holster, flipped it, grabbed it backward, and began using the butt to pound the knife blade into the mortar.

Several times he paused as bullets hammered the wall around him to return a few cursory shots, just to keep Larry and the girls occupied so they wouldn't suspect what he was up to. Otherwise he hammered the pistol butt against the knife handle, chipping the loose, brittle mortar out of the cracks around the stones.

As the light grew, chasing shadow into the room's corners, the mortar chunks piled up around Longarm's boots.

The slugs continued hammering the jailhouse, sparking off the iron bars and pummeling the stout wooden door. Longarm felt one ricochet tear along his left shoulder, while another burned his left ear lobe.

Still, he continued hammering the knife into the mortar.

After what seemed an hour but was probably only ten minutes, he'd chipped out an inch-deep line around the new stones.

He returned several shots in the direction of Vernon Wade's shop, noting that the dwarf's stout, dead body had nearly been shredded by flying lead. Then he dropped to his butt at the base of the wall, raised both his feet, and slammed the heels of his boots against the new stones inside the ragged circle of freshly hammered mortar.

Suddenly, the rifles fell silent.

Longarm froze.

Larry said in a consternated tone just loud enough for Longarm to hear, "What the hell's he's doin' in there?"

"Reckon we oughta check it out?" asked one of the girls.

"No," Longarm grunted, turning his head to one side. "Just keep shooting, damnit."

Larry said something Longarm couldn't hear, then,

"Wanda, Aubrey—cover me. I'm gonna wander over, see if he's got the coffee pot on."

Panic shot through Longarm's veins as sweat dribbled through the film of mortar dust on his rough-hewn cheeks. He drew a deep breath, then rocked toward the wall, ramming the heels of his cavalry boots forward.

His heels smashed against the wall, sending lightning bolts of pain up his legs and into his knees. The stones held firm.

Outside, spurs chinged. The chings grew louder as Loony Larry approached the jailhouse.

Chapter 17

Once more, Longarm rocked straight back on his butt, lifting his boots high above his belly.

"Hey, Longarm!" Loony Larry called from outside the jailhouse. "What the hell you doin' in there?"

With a harsh grunt, Longarm brought both feet forward, heels out, and pushing up with his hands, slammed his boots into the middle of the stones inside the ragged circle of old chinking. Several of the center stones gave, bending out and falling back with a raucous thunder of clattering rock.

"What the hell was that?" Larry said. Again, Longarm could hear the man's spurs ching as he moved toward the front door.

Longarm drew another deep breath and rammed both his feet once more against the remaining rocks. They burst away from the others around them and clattered down with those already dislodged, straight out into the alley behind the jailhouse.

Dust wafted and mortar sifted down through the four-by-three-foot hole. Hazy copper sunlight shone through the ragged opening.

Longarm turned and grabbed his Winchester as the silhouette of a hatted head appeared in the window to the left of the front door. He pushed onto his knees, shouldered the rifle, and fired, dislodging Loony Larry's hat as the crazy killer ducked.

Longarm fired another round, which plunked into the casing at the window's bottom, then dropped, thrust his head through the jagged hole in the wall, and kicked himself through with his feet, dragging the Winchester along behind him.

He was nearly through when two rifle blasts sounded from inside the building, the first hammering the wall just above the hole, the other slicing an icy burn along the top of Longarm's left knee. Gritting his teeth against the pain, Longarm threw himself sideways to the right of the hole, clutching his knee and catching his breath.

"He's gone out the back!" Loony Larry shouted, his voice cracking with exasperation. "He's gone out the back, goddamnit! Spread out, you girls!"

Longarm scrambled to his feet, his grazed knee dribbling blood down his shin and shooting fiery pain up and down his leg. He limped to the jailhouse's west rear corner and edged a look up the gap between the jailhouse and the harness shop. A Winchester snaked around the front of the jailhouse, and Loony Larry's hatless head followed.

Longarm snapped up his own rifle and fired two rounds, both slugs hammering off the side of the stone building as Larry pulled his head back with a shrill curse. Beyond the gap, Longarm saw three of the girls spread out, holding rifles, as they ran into the street.

Longarm bolted across the gap and up the alley behind several buildings, limping on his bad knee, blood soaking his pants leg. The sun was up now, casting a lemon glow across the sky behind him. The town was silent except for a barking dog and the thumps of running feet and trilling spurs around him, and Loony Larry yelling behind him, "Get that son of a bitch! I want his fucking *head*!"

A rifle cracked behind Longarm, the slug plunking into a wagon wheel leaning against a shed. Running and cursing with each painful step, Longarm glanced over his right shoulder. Loony Larry was sprinting toward him, holding his smoking Winchester in both hands across his chest, eyes wide and glassy. At the same time, Longarm heard running footsteps and trilling spurs emanating from the other side of an adobe brick building just ahead.

He approached the back of what appeared to be a blacksmith shop; split firewood was stacked against the rear wall. He flinched as Larry, running toward him, triggered another shot, which whistled past Longarm's right ear to plunk into the woodpile behind him.

Meanwhile, the thump and ching of boots and spurs rose louder from the other side of the blacksmith shop. The rifle-wielding Diamond girls were about to cut him off. In less than a minute, he'd be surrounded.

Ordinarily, a passel of girls wouldn't be all that disconcerting, but he'd seen the way these gals could shoot.

He glanced up at the roof above the woodpile—his only chance of escape, or at least a chance to buy himself some time. As Aubrey Diamond rounded the corner of the blacksmith shop, holding a rifle in both her gloved hands, a red neckerchief buffeting around her neck, Longarm set his jaws against the pain in his knee and bolted forward.

He used his left foot to spring off the chopping block, propelling himself up the shop's brick wall to the top of the woodpile, landing on his feet, the logs wobbling precariously beneath his boots.

Quickly, without turning to look behind but hearing Larry laugh and Aubrey shout, "We got him!" he tossed his Winchester onto the roof above his head, then reached up and grabbed the roof's lip with both hands.

Behind him and below rose the tooth-gnashing rasp of a cocking lever. His skin crawled as he sensed Loony Larry drawing a bead on him. Throwing himself onto the roof and rolling, he heard two rifles bark below and turned to see both slugs chewing at the shake shingles overhanging the roof's lip before screaming skyward.

"Goddamnit!" Loony Larry barked. "Get down here, goddamnit, you fuckin' lawdog. There ain't nowhere for you to go—can't you *see* that?"

Longarm rolled toward the edge of the roof, grabbed his Winchester's barrel, then rolled back toward the roof's middle, well out of sight from below. Gaining a knee and racking a shell into the Winchester's breech, he paused, breathing hard, again feeling the wetness basting his lower left leg.

The killer had a point. He'd bought himself some time and high ground, but there wasn't anywhere for him to go . . .

Or was there?

To the east lay the stone roof of the jailhouse, with no other buildings beyond it. To the west, however, a dozen or so roofs jutted skyward, one behind the other and probably no farther than twenty feet apart. Most were flat and abutted on the main street end by high false fronts.

"Where the hell is he?" Wanda cried from below.

"Up there!"

"What the hell's he doin' up there?"

"Dyin'!" Larry barked. "You girls step back and cover me, damnit!"

Hunkered low on one knee, his Winchester resting across his thigh, Longarm stretched his gaze over the end of the blacksmith shop's roof. Hats and oval-shaped faces appeared as the four sisters stepped back away from the shop, lifting their chins to peer up at the roof.

Longarm dropped to his belly and continued staring over the end of the roof. Someone grunted and logs rattled. Two hands curled over the lip of the roof, the left clad in a black leather glove, the right wearing a blood-speckled white bandage.

Longarm snugged the Winchester to his cheek, aimed, and fired.

K-blam!

The slug tore through the bandage on Loony Larry's right hand, about where Longarm had drilled him before.

A shrill, animalistic scream rose so loudly the dog that had been barking stopped suddenly. Both hands dropped back over the lip of the roof. The wood clattered again, followed by the thud of a body hitting the ground.

"Larry!" Aubrey cried.

"There he is!" Wanda shouted. She'd backed into the brush a good thirty yards from the shop. She snapped her rifle to her shoulder.

Longarm pushed to his feet as the girl drilled a round past his left ear. As Larry cursed and sobbed and Wanda and the other girls scuffed around trying to draw a bead on Longarm, he stepped back to the east side of the roof, then sprinted forward, heading west.

Another bullet whined past him as, ignoring the pain in his knee, he increased his speed as he neared the edge of the blacksmith shop roof, lifting his knees high, scissoring his arms. The sandy gap between the shop and the other building to the west yawned before him, strewn with yellowed newpapers, tin cans, and deer bones.

Longarm kicked off the edge of the blacksmith shop, sailed up and over the gap, spreading his arms, his rifle in his right hand, and hit the other roof with about two feet to spare.

Wanda shouted something, but Longarm couldn't hear because he was already sprinting across the shake-shingled roof before him, then finding himself airborne once again, leaping the gap, watching the brown grass and sand and a dilapidated wheelbarrow pass below him.

He hit the next roof with a grunt, his grazed knee buckling. He landed on his right shoulder and rolled, tarred timbers grunting and sighing beneath him as he raised his bloody knee to stem the pain. He choked on the wafting dust, kicking a tumbleweed snagged on a kid's torn kite from around his feet, then gained his good leg.

Rifles barked. Girls shouted. Larry cursed hoarsely. Boots thumped quickly, grinding gravel and hammering boardwalks.

Judging by the sounds, Loony Larry and the Diamond gals were spreading out around Longarm as they tried to follow him up the street.

Longarm sucked air through his teeth, stood, and peered west. The next roof was a little higher, so he had to kick himself up off the edge of this roof or he wouldn't make it. He sucked back the pain in his knee and ran across the roof, setting his boots at the edge and springing off his toes.

He hadn't gotten as much lift as he'd wanted. He caught the edge of the roof by only his arms, and dangled out over the lip like fresh bait on a hook.

The girls shouted excitedly and several slugs chewed the boards around his flailing legs as, cursing and setting his teeth, he hoisted himself up and onto the roof. He rolled clear of the edge as several more slugs plunked into the wall behind him.

As he readied himself for another leap, he heard Loony Larry barking orders and saw three of the girls running off across the street to his right, but with heads turned toward him, eyes pinched with fury. Longarm triggered a couple of shots in their direction, hoping to plink one or two to even the odds a little, but his bullets only plunked dust at their feet.

As lead threaded the air around him, Longarm leaped to the next building, squeezed off a couple more shots, then leaped to the next. He leaped one more, landed on his heels, and, sucking air through his teeth as his left knee throbbed, sprinted forward.

Another gap slipped away behind and below him, a large, brown dog barking furiously up at him, hackles raised. Longarm switched his gaze from the dog to the roof growing before him, and groaned with dread.

It was a slightly pitched, shake-shingled, rickety roof from which a tin chimney protruded. Several of the shakes were missing, and Longarm could see through to the hay-strewn floor of the dilapidated, apparently abandoned stable.

The roof didn't look like it could hold a sparrow, much less a 210-pound lawman holding a rifle and wearing a six-shooter and flying toward it like a human cannonball.

He hit the roof feet-first, then dropped forward onto his elbows. The shingles and joists rocked beneath him like a boat on choppy seas, and then it steadied.

Longarm raised his right knee, intending to crawl forward, but a sickening crunch and a snap sounded, and the roof sank out from beneath him. He suddenly found himself airborne once more, tumbling straight down through the stable's misty shadows, vaguely aware of the smell of rotting hay and bird shit.

"Jesuzzzz Keeee-*riist*!" he heard himself mutter, watching the floor rise quickly while shingles and chunks of rotten joists dropped along beside him.

The floor came up hard against his chest and belly, and he gave an enormous grunt as the air exploded from his lungs and his face slammed into the musty straw. His left knee barked like a dog in a steel trap, and his ears rang from the concussion.

But lifting his face, he was surprised to feel anything at all. If it hadn't been for the good eight or nine inches of straw covering this part of the barn floor, he'd have cheated Loony Larry out of the kill, though his head would no doubt be heading for the Denver Federal Building in a wooden box.

As the ringing in his ears subsided and he spat straw and dust from his mouth, coughing, he heard footsteps and heavy breathing off to his right, toward the front of the barn. A man laughed with unbridled glee, and through the missing bricks in the front wall, Longarm saw Dixon running toward the double doors.

Longarm groaned again as he climbed onto his hands and knees, scooping his rifle out of the straw. One of the doors opened with a loud scrape and squawk, and Loony Larry bolted through the opening, mouth and eyes wide as he laughed and aimed his rifle straight out from his right hip.

The fool didn't seem to mind that he was silhouetted

by the open door behind him. He swung the Winchester to his left and, howling madly, the ends of his snow-white mustache jostling, began firing blindly into the barn's shadows, the slugs plunking the walls and stall partitions and pinging off a metal tub hanging on a floor joist.

Clutching his rifle in his right hand, Longarm sprang off his heels and, as slugs chewed into the hard-packed floor behind him, dove behind a stock trough. He came up, extending the Winchester over the top of the trough, as Larry continued howling like a lobo while triggering shots toward the wall to Longarm's left.

The crazy killer's rifle hammer clicked, empty, and he continued howling through the wafting powder smoke as he slowly lowered the barrel. Then he gave one last celebratory whoop and dropped his voice several notches and growled through gritted teeth, "Somebody fetch my hatchet."

"That's a might premature, Larry," Longarm said mildly, drawing a bead on the killer's chest.

Loony Larry grunted, his face suddenly a mask of horror as, backing toward the opening, he dropped the Winchester and reached across his belly for the pistol on his left hip.

Longarm fired twice.

Both slugs took the killer through his chest, lifting him two feet up and pitching him straight back out the doors. He landed in the street with a heavy thump and a loud fart, knocking the right door wide with a reverberating shudder and a rake of dry hinges.

All Longarm could see of him now between the open doors were his boots—heels down, toes up. Loony Larry's feet shook as though they'd been struck by lightning.

"Larry!" Aubrey screamed. "Oh, God, Larry baby!"

Longarm glanced to his left. There was a small, partly open door in the barn's west wall. Pushing off his bloody knee, he made for the door as several pairs of running feet thumped up around the barn's front doors, heading toward the dying Larry Dixon while Aubrey sobbed and cried his name.

Longarm bolted out the door and, quickly thumbing fresh cartridges into his rifle, ran up along the stable's west wall. At the front, he paused, hearing boot scuffs and curses and cries from the direction of the barn doors.

Drawing a breath, he bolted around the corner, turned sharply right, and stopped, holding the Winchester in both hands at three Diamond gals spread out in front of Loony Larry over whose bloody corpse hunkered the golden-haired Aubrey. She sobbed as she cradled Larry's pink-crowned head in her arms.

"Hold it, ladies."

Wanda jerked her head toward him, holding a carbine one-handed, aimed at the barn, her men's boots spread a little more than shoulder-width apart. The other three girls turned toward him, also. Aubrey stared up at him through teary blue eyes. Her rifle lay beside her; two ivory-gripped Colts jutted from shoulder holsters on each side of her full, deep cleavage, yawning up from a wine red blouse and pinto vest.

Wanda's eyes narrowed with cunning. "You wouldn't kill three beautiful young women, would you, Longarm? A man like you, who does so appreciate the fairer sex?"

"It'd break my heart," Longarm allowed, "but my heart's been broken before. Drop those shootin' irons or go the way of Loony Larry."

Silence.

The girls studied him. Slowly, Aubrey straightened,

sniffing back tears and dropping her hands to her sides, the pearl grips of those Colts angling out from her half-exposed breasts, which, Longarm couldn't help noting, were a tad larger than Wanda's.

They'd all turned to face him now, hat brims shading their faces from the sun angling up over the barn, shoving a wedge of purple shade into the street.

The corners of Wanda's wide mouth rose as she said huskily, "I'm betting he can't do it."

"Well, you'd know," Lilly said. She was the only one in a dress—a blue silk affair with pleated skirts. Beneath the hem, her scuffed boots protruded. She held her Winchester in both gloved hands across her chest. "You bedded him."

The dark-haired Cassie, shorter than the rest and wearing skintight torn and faded denims, dropped her eyes toward Longarm's crotch. "Wouldn't mind wrestlin' that viper my ownself." She chuckled. "Too bad we gotta kill him."

As the other three girls slid their eyes to Wanda, she held that knowing smile and shook her head slowly, throwing her shoulders back so that her nipples pushed out from behind her shirt. "I don't think he can do it."

"Don't," Longarm warned, edging his rifle barrel slowly from left to right and back again, keeping his finger taut against the trigger, his eyes hard.

Aubrey dipped her chin to her chest, dropped her eyes to her breasts, then looked up once more to Longarm. "Nope." She smiled. "I don't think he can, either."

Longarm kept his eyes on the girls, but in the periphery of his vision he could see the dog that had been barking at him before peering around the stable's far corner and whining anxiously.

Wanda and Aubrey moved at almost the same time,

179

Wanda swinging her rifle toward Longarm, Aubrey snaking her hands across her chest to grab the ivory grips of her .45s.

Longarm had already made up his mind about what he had to do and, pretty as they were, Wanda and Aubrey were the first to spin around, screaming, as his lead sliced through them, and to tumble in the hay- and manure-strewn dust.

Lilly, surprisingly fast, was able to squeeze a shot off, but the slug plunked into the stable's brick wall as Longarm threw himself off his left shoulder and came up firing and levering the Winchester until Lilly and Cassie, too, were punched back off their heels to tumble in the dust already splattered with their sisters' blood.

Propped on his elbows, cocked Winchester angled up from his shoulder, Longarm squinted through the sifting dust and powder smoke. None of the girls was moving. He'd killed them fast and clean, which was more than they deserved.

As he gained his good knee and groaned as he put weight on the bad one, he saw Veron Wade walking toward him along the middle of the street. Around Wade, wary-eyed shop owners peered out from windows and doorways, while several doves in colorful wrappers and night ribbons stared down from a wrought-iron balcony, looking none too happy about being awakened from their hard-earned slumbers.

"Holy shit!" Wade said as, rubbing the back of his head, where Larry had laid him out with his rifle butt, he inspected the carnage around him. Larry himself lay flat on his back, bleeding from the two holes in his chest, mustache glowing in the golden morning sunshine.

Wade glanced at Longarm. "I seen the dwarf, or what's left of him. How'd Doyle fair?"

The lawman shook his head. "I reckon you'll be tendin' Doyle for the last time, Mr. Wade."

The undertaker–barber shook his head as he cast his disconsolate gaze at the bloody, dusty girls staring up glassy-eyed from the crimson dirt around them. "I realize you had to do what you done, but what a shame . . . blowin' the wicks of such lovely gals."

"Lovely on the outside—I couldn't agree more with that." Longarm sank down on a water trough and, with a heavy sigh, removed his neckerchief and began wrapping it around his bloody knee. "But never judge a book by its cover"—he gritted his teeth as he pulled the neckerchief taut—"nor a woman by her pretty tits."

Leaving those words of wisdom to settle with the dust and gun smoke behind him, he got his knee stitched, saddled the buckskin, and while Vernon Wade was busily building coffins, started back to Denver.

Watch for

Longarm and the Happiness Killers

the 357th novel in the exciting LONGARM
series from Jove

Coming in August!

****

And don't miss these Longarm Omnibus Editions
—The first four novels in the LONGARM series—

Available from Jove in August!

Longarm Double #1: Deputy U.S. Marshal
  Novel 1. Longarm
  Novel 2. Longarm on the Border

Longarm Double #2: Longarm of the Law
  Novel 3. Longarm and the Avenging Angels
  Novel 4. Longarm and the Wendigo

GIANT-SIZED ADVENTURE FROM
AVENGING ANGEL LONGARM.

BY TABOR EVANS

2006 Giant Edition:

**LONGARM AND THE
OUTLAW EMPRESS**

2007 Giant Edition:

**LONGARM AND THE
GOLDEN EAGLE SHOOT-OUT**

penguin.com

BERKLEY WESTERNS TAKE OFF LIKE A SHOT

Lyle Brandt
Peter Brandvold
Jack Ballas
J. Lee Butts
Jory Sherman
Ed Gorman
Mike Jameson

Don't miss the best Westerns from Berkley.

penguin.com

M10G0907

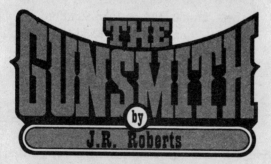